The Mysterious

Volume.

Sophia Reeve

Alpha Editions

This edition published in 2024

ISBN : 9789361473807

Design and Setting By
Alpha Editions
www.alphaedis.com
Email - info@alphaedis.com

Contents

He waved his hand for St. Ledger to follow him, and left the cabin. Frederick likewise retired, leaving the Lieutenant highly incensed at the reproof he had received, and the favourable reception given to the indigent St. Ledger.

Descended from an ancient and wealthy family—an only child—Harland had early been taught to regard merit only in proportion to the birth of the individual; and whilst the actions of his ancestors were recited to raise an emulation in his bosom, they implanted a pride, the partial fondness of his parents but too much tended to increase. Thus regarding himself as superior to the generality of mankind, he expected an observance and obedience few were willing to pay. The Captain's profession of friendship to St. Ledger, after he had so openly avowed his disapprobation of that youth, he looked on as an insult offered to himself, and as such determined to show his resentment by treating him with every mark of contempt in his power. This behaviour, however, failed in the desired effect; and, instead of degrading St. Ledger, was the means of gaining him the notice and protection of the other officers. By the austerity of his manners, Harland had long since rendered himself the object of their dislike; the injustice of his behaviour was therefore exaggerated in their opinion, and, independently of the Captain's avowed partiality, or the interesting manners of the young adventurer, inclined them to regard him with sentiments of commiseration and friendship.

Already had St. Ledger been six weeks on board, during which time the Captain had repeatedly, but vainly, urged him to declare who he was; neither could he be induced to appear when any strangers visited that gentleman; when one day, being importuned by Frederick to accompany them to the house of a friend, he hesitatingly acknowledged it was not safe for him to be seen.

"Not safe, St. Ledger?" repeated the Captain. "Of what action can you have been guilty, that like a midnight assassin, you should thus dread the observation of civilized society?"

"None, Captain," answered St. Ledger firmly. "But the criminal is not the only one who has cause for fear. He who meets the hand of the assassin is in equal danger as he who gives the blow."

"Well, St. Ledger," returned the Captain, "I yield to your reasons, whatever they may be. I entertain too good an opinion of you to think you guilty of any crime which could render you undeserving of the protection I have afforded. When you have known me longer, you may perhaps find me more worthy of your confidence."

St. Ledger felt relieved by their departure, though hurt at the reproach he thought the Captain's last words implied.

For that gentleman, he sunk into a reverie as soon as he was seated in the barge; which Frederick, whose imagination was equally employed in conjectures respecting St. Ledger, never thought of interrupting; and on being landed they silently pursued their way till they arrived at the quay, when Frederick suddenly exclaimed—"I cannot form an idea who, or what St. Ledger is. Above the generality of mankind I must think him."

"I have indeed," said the Captain, "rarely seen his equal, and would freely give a hundred guineas to know who he is, or his reason for wishing to be concealed. If he would intrust me with the secret, it might perhaps be in my power to prove a greater friend to him than I am at present."

The concluding sentence brought them to the place of their destination. On being announced, a gentleman, who was seated with their invitor, hastily rose, and, eagerly surveying the Captain, exclaimed—

"Does my memory deceive me; or is it my friend Crawton I have again the pleasure of beholding?"

"I was once known by that name," answered the Captain, with emotion; "but at present bear that of Howard."

"Tell me," said the other, with quickness, "were you ever acquainted with one Talton, of Brighthelmstone?"

"Brighthelmstone!—Talton!" repeated the Captain, taking his hand—"Surely it is.—It is my old friend Talton himself! Yet scarcely can I credit the existence of one I thought long since numbered with the dead."

"I wonder not at your entertaining the idea," said Mr. Talton. "The years that have intervened since last we beheld each other, and a variety of circumstances, might justly give rise to such a supposition."

The pleasure experienced by the Captain at thus meeting a man whose friendship had once constituted a considerable portion of his happiness, diffused itself to the bosoms of all, and some time elapsed ere he thought of asking an explanation of the occurrences by which he had been induced to believe the death of his friend.

On Frederick and their entertainer likewise expressing a wish to hear his relation, Mr. Talton readily consented to gratify their curiosity.

"Though I would not, my friends," he continued, "have you expect to hear any thing extraordinary in my history, as there is not any circumstance in the whole, but what daily and hourly happens to hundreds of my fellow-beings, or that can render it interesting to any but the ear of friendship.

"I believe, Howard, I need not recapitulate the circumstances which eighteen years since induced me to leave England; as I doubt not you well remember the death of my guardian, and the villany of my steward in Barbadoes, who, on that event, endeavoured to defraud me of the property I inherited from my mother.

"Our voyage was tempestuous and tedious; and on landing at Barbadoes, I found Johnson regarded as the legal possessor of my lands. I carried sufficient proofs of my identity and the validity of my claim; but, irritated to the highest degree, declined an application to law as too tedious in its redress, and determined personally to assert and enforce my right.

"I accordingly went, accompanied by some friends, who had in vain endeavoured to dissuade me from such a procedure, and was admitted into the presence of Johnson, whom I accused with all the vehemence of ungoverned rage, and declared my intention of maintaining possession from that period. He heard me with an affectation of surprise; and then, with the greatest effrontery, said—'You the son of the late honourable Alric Talton, and the owner of these plantations! This impudence exceeds all I ever witnessed! No, sir, the son of my late master is too well known to me to admit of this imposition. From him I purchased these possessions, and from him, from you, and all the world, I will now withhold them.'

"Driven nearly to madness by this impudent assertion, I still insisted on the justness of my claim, and menaced him with the utmost severity of the law; whilst he in return pretended to treat me as an impostor, and threatened to have me punished accordingly.

"My friends finding the inutility of the attempt, proposed my returning to Bridgetown, and seeking redress from the Governor. This I told them they were welcome to do, but I should remain where I was; and, finding me obstinate to my purpose, they at last set out for town without me.

"As soon as they were gone, Johnson summoned two European servants, and commanded them to search my pockets; and, whilst my arms were confined by his order, I had the mortification to see those papers concerning his stewardship, and which as of most consequence in my cause I carried about my person, torn to pieces and consumed! Then regarding me with a sarcastic grin—'As you are determined to remain here, young man, it is as little as I can do to accommodate you with an apartment; though, perhaps, it may not prove altogether agreeable to your wishes.'

"He then ordered me to be conducted to a room he named, and which I afterwards found was used as a place of confinement to those slaves who failed in their attempts for liberty. My arms were there unbound, and I was left to the solitary comfort of a bed of reeds. The first violence of passion subsiding, I perceived the folly of my late behaviour; and, as I doubted not my friends would effect my liberation, I determined, if possible, to rectify the errors my rage had occasioned; and I had still sufficient proofs remaining, I doubted not, to bring Johnson to justice.

"According to my expectations, my friends, the next day, came to Johnson's, and on being refused any satisfactory intelligence respecting me, applied to the Governor, who issued an order, in consequence of which my villanous steward was obliged to release me, or stand indicted for my murder. A formal process of law was then commenced against him; the cause finally brought to trial; and, as my witnesses and proofs were indisputable, the verdict pronounced in my favour. But the crafty villain effectually screened himself from punishment by the evidence of his two servants, who positively swore their master had, previously to my arrival, purchased the plantations of a man who assumed my name; and that they were witnesses to the deeds, which were accordingly produced.

"The behaviour of Johnson in destroying the papers relative to the stewardship, and the question—where could he honestly have amassed money sufficient for the purchase—effectually proved the falsity of this account: but as I had recovered my right, and could bring no witnesses of his conduct, I desisted from farther prosecution.

"Johnson, thus cleared from intentional fraud, unquestioned master of the money he had amassed during his illegal tenure of the plantations, purchased one adjoining mine, and proved such a troublesome neighbour, that for five years I had occasion for all my forbearance and circumspection, to avoid a continual course of law-suits. During that time my affairs in England had been very little attended to; and as my overseer was a man on whose integrity I could rely, I determined to pay a visit to my native country. I accordingly came to England, passed some months at Bath, and went to Brighthelmstone, for the purpose of visiting you, to whom I had repeatedly written: but on my arrival there, was informed no person of the name of Crawton resided in the place; nor could I gain the least intelligence respecting you.

"Having settled my affairs to my satisfaction, I again returned to Barbadoes, where I passed ten years more without any thing material occurring; except that Johnson had the impudence to propose an alliance between me and his daughter, a girl of sixteen; but the offer was rejected with the disdain it merited. He soon after died, and I once more visited England, where some events which have happened, will most probably induce me to fix my future residence. I went to the continent about six weeks since, to settle accompts with my correspondents, whence I yesterday returned; and happy indeed do I deem myself in the discovery of this afternoon."

A more minute recapitulation of incidents beguiled the time till the period of the Captain's return on board, when he parted from his friend, who promised to pass the ensuing day with him.

CHAPTER II.

The cheerfulness which had animated the countenance of the Captain, deserted him when he quitted the presence of Mr. Talton; a deep dejection succeeded, and the half-stifled sigh evinced the recollection of events painful to remembrance. Frederick vainly endeavoured to divert his attention, but his voice had lost its wonted influence; nor, when returned on board, was the interesting St. Ledger more successful in dispelling the saddened cloud from his brow. The Captain regarded him for some time in mournful silence, then hastily bade him good night, and retired to his cabin, whence he was summoned in the morning, on the arrival of Mr. Talton. His pallid countenance sufficiently showed how ill he had passed the night, nor could his efforts to assume a cheerful ease succeed.

Mr. Talton beheld the alteration with concern, and took the occasion of his absence to ask Frederick the reason of it.

"Alas, Sir," replied Frederick, "I cannot resolve your question; my uncle is frequently—nay generally dejected; but with the cause I am unacquainted."

"I know," said Mr. Talton, "that early in life he experienced unhappiness from his family; yet, surely after so many years have elapsed—Yet it may: the enmity of his brother was too deeply rooted to yield to time—And shall I own my surprise at finding the son of that brother on board the Argo? Excuse my curiosity, young gentleman, but are you here with or without the knowledge and approbation of your father?"

Frederick sighed. "My father, sir, knows and approves of my being here."

"—Are you," said Mr. Talton, after a moment's pause, "acquainted with the cause of their quarrel!"

"I am not, sir," answered Frederick. "From my earliest remembrance the unhappy disagreement between my uncle and father has existed: and to such excess did my father carry his inveteracy, he would not permit even the name of his brother to be mentioned in his presence: and, except by name, I scarcely knew such a person existed. My early propensity for the sea, which my father in vain strove to eradicate, and the haughty ungenerous disposition of my elder brother, brought me continual anger and chastisement, till I was nearly fourteen; when I accompanied my father to a race near Salisbury; and, where my uncle, without knowing who I was, saved my life, by extricating me from an unruly horse, which my curiosity to see the course had tempted me to mount. He afterwards accompanied me to my father, who was beginning coolly to thank him, when he recalled to mind, his brother in my preserver, and rage, in an instant, took possession of every faculty. He struck me down, and severely should I have suffered for the involuntary offence, if my uncle had not interposed—desiring to speak with him in private. After a conference of about half an hour, they returned; my father's brow still exhibited a formidable frown; and, as he entered, I heard him say, 'If you take him—you take him entirely: nor, after he is once under your guidance, shall I think myself necessitated to provide for him in the least respect. I have other children, more deserving my care esteem: you have none—and, if you like, may adopt him; your dispositions are exactly similar!'

"My uncle smiled at the latter part of his speech, and asked if I would go to sea with him? I readily acceded to the offer, and that very evening bade adieu to a parent, whose harshness rendered him an object of dread, and repressed every sentiment of filial affection. My uncle wrote twice to my father; the first letter he answered, saying, he was glad I behaved to his satisfaction; and since that time, all intercourse has again ceased. My uncle, at his own expense, equipped me for the sea, and has ever supplied my wants with unbounded generosity."

At this moment the Captain re-entered.

Mr. Talton beheld with concern his encreasing melancholy, and for some time strove to divert it; but finding all his efforts ineffectual, he at last said—

"What, Howard, is the cause of the dejection which oppresses you? That cloud on your brow is by no means flattering to my present visit, and but little accords with your professions of friendship, or the honest pleasure that yesterday enlivened your features. I know you too well to think it occasioned by any trivial circumstances: what then, my friend, is the reason?—Your wife, you say, is well."

"Name her not, I entreat," replied the Captain, severely hurt at the reproach of his friend. "She is, indeed, the source of all my unhappiness!"

"The source of your unhappiness!" repeated Mr. Talton. "Surely, Howard, I do not understand you, or your sentiments are strangely altered since the time I gave the lovely Ellenor Worton to your arms. Then—"

"Oh, Talton," interrupted the Captain, "cease this subject, I conjure you. Ellenor Worton! My God, what ideas does that name recall! Yes, far above my life I prized her: but those days are for ever fled! I am wretched, and she is now a friendless fugitive in a merciless world!"

"What mean you, Howard?" asked Mr. Talton. "There is a mystery in your words I do not understand."

"Then I will explain them," returned the Captain. "Your friendship, your honour, I have proved; and when you hear my tale, you will not wonder why, on beholding the friend of my earlier days, instead of smiles, my countenance should thus wear the semblance of sorrow and regret."

Frederick would here have retired, as imagining what his uncle had to impart, he might wish should only reach the knowledge of his friend; but the Captain bade him resume his seat.—"From my errors," he added, "you may learn to avoid their attending unhappiness."

Frederick obeyed; and the Captain, addressing Mr. Talton, continued.

"At the commencement of our acquaintance, I believe, I informed you I was a younger son, brought up to the sea, and deprived of the fortune I expected, by the marriage of my elder brother. I was, at the period of that marriage, seventeen. Sir Thomas Gratton, the father of the lady my brother espoused, refused his consent to their union, unless Arthur's fortune were made adequate to the one he gave his daughter; and my father, overcome by the entreaties of my brother, and perhaps dazzled with the idea of his marrying an heiress with three thousand a year, complied so far as to resign two-thirds of his estate (which was equal to that of Sir Thomas) on the day of marriage, with the reversion of the remainder at his decease.

"Arthur, in return, secretly, but solemnly, promised to present me and William, our other brother, with ten thousand pounds each, on our coming of age, or at the death of his father-in-law. William died the ensuing year, as did Sir Thomas in less than nine months after.

"My brother had hitherto expressed the greatest affection for me: I stood godfather for my Frederick here, and every thing bore the appearance of harmony and cordiality; till, being at an assembly at Lavington, my ill fortune led me, through whim, ridicule, and the gaiety of youth, to pay particular attentions to a Miss Deborah Tangress, a maiden lady nearly fifty, noted for every unamiable quality, ugliness, and riches! Little did I think the folly of that evening would have created me so many years of misery!

"Pleased with the attentions and compliments she thought serious, and despising the delicacy requisite in her sex, she sent proposals to my father, offering to resign herself and fortune to my disposal. I was laughing at the effects of my evening's mirth, when my brother entered the room; my father gave him the letter, and, smiling, observed, he thought Miss Deborah had completed her character.

"'I cannot so readily conceive the occasion of your immoderate laughter, Edward,' said my brother: 'the offer is advantageous, far beyond what you have a right to expect; and, instead of ridiculing, I think you rather ought to accept it with thankfulness.'

"'Accept it with thankfulness!' I repeated. 'What, and chain myself to such an ugly old——'.

"'As to her being old and ugly,' interrupted my brother, 'it is of very little consequence. You will recollect, sir, she has an ample fortune, and you have none!'

"'Not so destitute as that, Arthur,' said my father: 'the fortune he is entitled to from your hands, though small, will render him so far independent that he may choose for himself.'

"'Excuse me, sir,' answered my brother, 'I cannot say I think myself obliged to give Edward a fortune from my own purse, especially when one so large as that Miss Tangress possesses is offered. If he have any regard for his own interest, he will accept it, and not look to me for future supplies. I have nearer ties; my children——.' "But excuse me, Talton, here is one"—(looking at Frederick, who appeared surprised and shocked at this account of his father) "too nearly interested to be pleased with this part of my narrative. Suffice it to say,—the mask was here thrown off by my brother, and I condemned to poverty! For the promise given to my father was merely verbal, and without witness, whilst the possessions of my father, in full confidence of Arthur's honour, had been secured to him by the strongest ties of the law.

"My father felt the stroke more severely than I did; he wept—and, in the bitterest anguish, asked pardon of heaven and me, for the step he had taken, and begged I would reconsider the proposal of Miss Tangress, before I absolutely rejected it. In all probability, he said, a few years would terminate her existence; I had no particular attachment to restrict me; and it would convey ease to his death-bed to know I was not only independent of my brother, but in a state of equal affluence.

"In the passion of the moment, this last consideration determined me; I complied—and in less than three weeks became the husband of Miss Tangress.

"The possession of her fortune, however, could not recompense me for her haughty wayward disposition. In her domestic arrangements she was tyrannical and parsimonious, and so truly capricious, that the most studied attentions to please could not twice succeed in the same particular. Certain I had not married for love, her rancorous disposition soon led her to resent, or rather to revenge, my want of affection. My expenditure became extravagance, my wants superfluous, and my acquaintance by far too general. As such, by the most pointed slights and insults, my friends were severally driven from my house; nor was even my father spared.

"I bore with the temper of my wife till human patience could sustain it no longer; and one day, after having been severely reproached with the favour she had conferred in uniting herself to a man not worth a shilling; I mounted my horse, and crossed the country to Brighthelmstone.

"The second night after my arrival there, I went to the ball given in honour of Sir Henry Beechton, where I became acquainted with you, and first saw the lovely Ellenor.

"To mention my admiration is needless: you are already well acquainted with it. To my anxious inquiries concerning her, the only intelligence I gained was—that she was an orphan of small fortune, and under the protection of the Hon. Mrs. Radnor. Fortune, however, had then lost its allurements. Ellenor shone with all the graces of a fabled goddess, which, added to the benignity that beamed in her eyes, and the ineffable sweetness of her manner, fixed her at once supremely in my heart. Impelled by love, I pursued the acquaintance; Ellenor owned her regard for me to her friend; and as neither that lady nor she had the least suspicion of my being married, (for, on my arrival at Brighthelmstone, I had taken my mother's name of Crawton, to prevent my wife from tracing me), my visits were welcomed with the greatest cordiality and friendship on the part of her protectress, and the sincerest affection by my Ellenor.

"It was then I fully experienced the wretchedness of my situation, in being united to Deborah. Reason and honour bade me combat with my passion, and fly from Ellenor. But in vain; each succeeding interview discovered new perfections, and by forcing a comparison, added to my love for her, and detestation for my wife. Hard was the conflict—but love prevailed: and I strove, by fallacious reasoning, to persuade myself, that my marriage with Miss Tangress was of no effect, as I was led into it by passion and revenge; and that an union with Ellenor, though contrary to the laws of my country, being founded on mutual affection, would not only be accepted in the eye of heaven, but acceded to as just, by the unprejudiced part of mankind.

"Meanwhile, I kept the secret buried in my breast. Ellenor, not mistrusting my account of myself or family, sought not for farther information than I gave; the banns were published in a village a few miles from Brighthelmstone, where, with your assistance, my friend, as father to my Ellenor, we were married!

"Of my happiness, you, Talton, were a witness; and the time flew with rapidity, till, by accident, I heard my father was dangerously ill; when filial affection for that best of parents, resumed its sway; and, taking a tender leave of Ellenor, I arrived at Howard Hall time enough to receive his last blessing.

"My father left me what his economy had saved since the discovery of my brother's sentiments; a few personal effects, his picture, with that of my mother, and her jewels. Inconsiderable as the bequest was, in comparison to the possessions devolved to Sir Arthur, he disputed my right to them; but as I prized them, not for their intrinsic value, but the affection of him who gave them, and, looking on him as the primary cause of my marrying Deborah, I not only refused to resign them, but upbraided him with his sordidness on that occasion. This produced a quarrel which has never been healed: he forswore—disowned me! This scene was followed by one nearly equal to it with my wife; which adding to my disgust, I directed my lawyer where to remit my small fortune, (for as I lived not with Deborah, I disdained all thoughts of hers) and once more returned to the arms of my Ellenor.

"Months again flew; when our happiness received its first shock by the sudden death of our invaluable friend Mrs. Radnor; and this was followed by your departure for the West Indies. Love, however, overcame these afflictions; my Ellenor became pregnant, and I was in expectation of soon being hailed by the name of father; when one day, sitting with my angel, fondly anticipating future felicities, the door was thrown open, and Deborah, accompanied by my lawyer, rushed into the room!

"To describe the scene which followed, is impossible: even now the recollection of it nearly maddens me! Deborah acted congenially to the fury of her character; aspersed my Ellenor, and reviled me with every opprobrious epithet the wildest passion, heightened by jealousy, could dictate; nor ceased—till Ellenor, overcome by the disclosure of the baleful secret, fainted in my arms; then, with the same violence as she entered, flew out of the room, followed by her companion, vowing to be revenged, though she expended her fortune in accomplishing it!

"At last my Ellenor recovered: not a single reproach at my conduct escaped her lips, but her countenance plainly showed the agony of her mind. Willing to lessen the idea of my guilt, which had been exaggerated by the frantic Deborah, I recapitulated the circumstances I have now related, and, with all the eloquence I was master of, pleaded the affection I entertained for her, as an excuse for the deceit I had practised. She heard me in silence; a convulsive sob swelled her bosom; and, on my again urging her forgiveness, she regarded me with a look of mingled anguish and despair. Tears at last relieved her, and she requested to be conducted to her chamber; I supported her there, and, leaving her to the care of her maid, returned to the parlour, my bosom filled with a sorrow and remorse that have never since deserted it! I was roused from reflections painful in the extreme, by a message from Deborah, demanding my presence, with which I was weak enough to comply, and for an hour and a half sustained the fury of her rage and reproaches, when, as neither would agree to the proposals of the other, we again parted. On my return home, I eagerly inquired after Ellenor. 'She is gone, sir!' said the girl, bursting into tears. 'Gone!' I repeated. 'How—when—where is she gone?' 'That, sir,' she answered, 'I know not. Soon after you went out, my lady sent Susan for a chaise and four, which, the moment it arrived, she entered, leaving this letter for you. Susan put in a few parcels, and followed her mistress; but where they are gone to, God only knows!'

"I seized the letter; and you may judge of what I felt when I perused it."

The Captain, with a sigh, drew a case from his bosom, and, taking out the letter, read as follows:

"I mean not, Edward, to upbraid you with an action, which, though it has involved your Ellenor in misery, was the offspring of affection; or, by unavailing complaints, add to the sorrow that already fills your bosom. No—rather let me speak peace to your mind, and, if possible, soften this, perhaps last, farewell! I have sustained the shock! Your real wife—oh, Edward, Edward!—But I will be calm.

"After the discovery of last night, honour, religion, virtue, forbid my continuance here. I am the child of misfortune; to stay, would make me the child of guilt! Justice likewise demands, that whilst your wife exists, you should think of Ellenor no otherwise than as a friend; I cannot say—forget me; that would be injustice to myself. No, Edward—pure has ever been my affection; and if Heaven should release you from your vows, remember the hand, the heart of Ellenor, may be demanded. Till then attempt not to discover me; the search would be fruitless. Justice demands the sacrifice, and it must be made! Yet how can I say—farewell! How tear myself from him on whose existence that of Ellenor depends; be merciful, Heaven—nor inflict a punishment past my power to support! Still let me stay—let me at least see my Edward, and hear him speak!—But it must not be. Oh, Edward, the punishment is just! You had your secrets, and I had mine!

"My hand is incapable of performing its office; I would, but cannot proceed. Oh, Edward! think of your Ellenor; doubt not my love—my constancy: and Heaven yet may make us happy!"

"You had your secrets, and I had mine! O God! what years of anxiety and painful conjecture, have those words occasioned!

"A stupefying horror at first pervaded my faculties: I sunk into a chair, and, but for the officious attentions of Mary, should have experienced a total—happy had it been a lasting insensibility!

"'Where can she be gone?' I faintly exclaimed, when recollection had regained sufficient power.

"'She cannot be gone far,' sobbed Mary. 'Perhaps, sir, you yet may overtake her.'

"The idea served effectually to rouse me: I commenced my search, and soon gained intelligence: a carriage, answerable to that I described, with a lady and her attendant in it, had been seen on the London road. To London I immediately directed my course; and at last descried a carriage, my sanguine hopes led me to think was that containing the sum of my earthly happiness: I instantly spurred my horse, when, owing to the badness of the road, or some other cause, he stumbled—fell, and threw me with violence over his head. I was stunned by the fall, found by some travellers, and, in a state of insensibility, conveyed to the nearest inn.

"The hurts I received were not very material; but the agitation of my mind at being thus prevented from pursuing Ellenor, brought on a fever which confined me to my apartment for nearly a fortnight. As soon as I was in a state to travel, I again pursued my way toward London, though with very little hope, after the time which had elapsed, of discovering her.

"For weeks after my arrival at the metropolis, I wandered about in the faint hope fortune might direct my steps to the place where she was secreted; when, one evening, returning to my lodging, I was surprised by the appearance of Deborah's equipage, who had likewise been seeking for, and at last traced me to London. She saw me ere I could enter the house, when, more than ever detesting the idea of an interview, I immediately removed to another part of the town.

"The next day I passed as usual in wandering about, and returned in the evening dejected and fatigued, when, taking up a book belonging to the hostess, a paper fell from it; it was a sonnet to Hope: but, good Heavens, think of my astonishment when I found it was the writing of my Ellenor! At first I discredited the evidence of my senses, till reiterated examinations convinced me I was not mistaken. I flew to the mistress of the house, and, in answer to my incoherent inquiries, gained intelligence, that she had left those apartments but a few days before I took them; that she had there been delivered of a son, and was then gone to reside in Caermarthen, her native county; though to what part, the hostess could not tell. To Caermarthen I determined to go, and accordingly the next morning commenced my journey; but all my search was indeed fruitless!

"At last, overcome by fatigue, preyed on by a fever occasioned by my repeated disappointments, and, to own the truth, not having money to prosecute my search, having expended that left me by my father, I was necessitated to retire to my habitation at Brighthelmstone, where Deborah again obtained information of me, and again laid me under the lash of her malignant power. Willingly would I have sought relief in a formal separation; but that she refused with the most contemptuous disdain, telling me I should never enjoy a portion of her wealth without her. I would then have resigned all pretensions to her fortune; but she started into phrensy, vowed she would follow me to the utmost extremity of the globe, and sooner deprive herself of every comfort in life, than leave me at liberty to renew an acquaintance with a woman I preferred to herself. Finding it in vain to gain her accordance to my proposal, I desisted from the attempt, and again commenced a search after Ellenor; Deborah, like my evil genius, still following me from place to place, till wearied, regardless of existence, and as the only means of escaping from her, I again went to sea. The interest of my friends gained me promotion; and fortune, by an influx of wealth during seventeen years, has been willing, as far as her power extends, to make me amends for the misery she has occasioned me in the loss of Ellenor, the continued torments I endure from Deborah, and the unkind neglect of my brother, whom I have seen but once since the death of my father.

"And here, Talton, I must apologize for my neglect to you. Your first letter, informing me you had regained your property, I received a few days preceding the discovery of my marriage with Deborah; but the distraction of my mind at that time prevented me from answering it. When I had in some degree regained my tranquillity, I wrote; but the person to whose charge I intrusted my packet, nearly two years after returned it, with the account that you were either dead, or had left the island; and as during that time, nor since, I never heard from you, I was induced to believe the former part of his intelligence.

"The pleasure I yesterday experienced on beholding you, for the time banished every other reflection; but no sooner did I quit you, than remembrance, with the keenest powers, revived every former scene, and added not only to my compunction for my injuries to—, but to my sorrow, for the irretrievable loss of my beloved Ellenor."

CHAPTER III.

Mr. Talton remained thoughtful some minutes after the Captain had ceased speaking; then addressing him—"If you were some years younger, Howard, I should censure you severely for your conduct; but as it is, and in consideration of the punishment you have already endured, I shall suspend my lecture! Poor Ellenor! It is strange, Howard, in the course of so many years you should never have gained any intelligence, nor met with the least circumstance from which you could judge of her destiny."

"It is strange, Talton. A few weeks back my nephew introduced a youth on board, whose appearance raised such emotions in my breast as I cannot attempt to describe. He was the exact resemblance of my Ellenor; his age too agrees with my son's, if living; but every hope was soon destroyed, his answers plainly proved he was not her child."

A sigh of regret here burst from the bosom of the Captain; nor could he refrain an impatient exclamation against the severity of his fate, in being thus deprived of those he regarded as the blessings of his existence.

"Though your life, Howard," said Mr. Talton, "has been rather out of the dull track of common occurrences, yet I would not have you think you have had more than your share of human ills; of those, believe me, all have an equal dispensation, and, sooner or later, feel the hand of adversity! As your morning of life has been clouded, you should, I think, look forward to a clear evening. You yet may find your Ellenor, and your son be restored, all your fondest desires could wish. You still have hope! Many, suffering afflictions, are bereaved of that blessing, by a fatal certainty of ill, where their happiness depends."

"Certainty of ill—" repeated the Captain—"Ah, Talton, am I not chained to a woman I detest, deprived of her I idolized, and a son whose endearments and attentions might have soothed the little sorrows of my bosom? But you are a bachelor, unrestrained by any ties which can justly interest the heart, and therefore cannot judge for me."

"Pardon me, my friend," returned Talton. "I speak not from conjecture; neither am I altogether unacquainted with those anxieties which have rendered you unhappy; and if you will listen to the tale of the woman I love, you may, perhaps, be convinced of the justness of my assertion."

The Captain bowed his consent—.

"Miss Holly, Howard, was an only daughter, and brought up by an old humourist of a father, whose idol she was, whilst she yielded every sense to his guidance. Many proposals of marriage were offered, but none thought worthy her acceptance by Mr. Holly, till he accidentally met with Sir Horace

Corbet, an old schoolfellow, and as great an oddity as himself, with whom he renewed his acquaintance; and an union was proposed between their children—agreed on, the writings drawn, and the wedding-day fixed, before the young people were acquainted with the least circumstance, or their sentiments respecting it, asked! Miss Holly received the mandate of her father, to regard Mr. Corbet as the husband he had selected, with the greatest distress; and at last informed him her affections were irrevocably fixed on another. But vain were her supplications and tears: the old gentleman was peremptory—and Miss Holly eloped!

"I shall not attempt to describe the rage of the fathers on this occasion; six months elapsed without their being able to discover the place of her retreat; when her aunt, who had for years estranged herself from all intercourse with the family, arrived at Holly seat, and, with great formality, acquainted her brother his daughter had taken refuge with her, and, hoping by that time his resentment had subsided, had engaged her to attempt a reconciliation. The old gentleman appeared delighted; a messenger was dispatched for her, and, on her arrival, she was received with every demonstration of joy and affection! The calm, however, was deceitful; for the next morning he led her to the chapel, where Sir Horace and his son were waiting, and there forced her to give her hand to the latter! Could happiness result from such an union?—Oh no! What followed might naturally have been expected; indifference on one side, disgust on the other.

Soon after the nuptials, Mrs. Corbet's aunt died; and, considering her niece highly injured by the measures which had been pursued, left her the whole of her fortune, amounting to thirty thousand pounds, independent of her husband. In less than a twelvemonth Mr. Holly died, leaving them eight thousand a year: Sir Horace survived his friend but a few weeks, and Sir Henry succeeded to nearly fifteen thousand a year more. Their decease, however, which a year before would have been the means of Lady Corbet's happiness, was then of no avail; the gentleman on whom her early affections had been placed, on hearing of her marriage, retired to France, where he literally died of a broken heart.

"Sir Henry now, uncontrolled by parental authority, yielded to the wildest passions of his heart. The mild dignity of his wife was disregarded, her beauty insufficient to restrain him from illicit connexions, and, whilst she was restricted with a parsimonious hand to her marriage settlement, she had the mortification of beholding immense property squandered on his worthless mistresses. As a landlord and master, Sir Henry was certainly beloved; but his character as a husband degenerated into that of a brutal tyrant.

"Soon after the decease of her father, Lady Corbet was delivered of a son, and in him (being deprived of all other) she concentrated her future happiness.

"On my first return from America, as I yesterday informed you, I passed some months at Bath, where I was introduced to Lady Corbet, and, had she been single, I should have said, Here Talton rest for ever!—as it was, nothing passed but what the strictest prude might have witnessed, though the censuring world imputed actions to me, I was innocent of, even in intention. Sir Henry was on an excursion with some friends, when I first became acquainted with his family; on his return, Lady Corbet presented me to him; he scarcely deigned a perceptible bow, but, throwing himself into a chair, called for his son, who was then about five years old, and, without once addressing me, amused himself in talking to, and answering his infantine questions. I regarded Lady Corbet with a look, I believe, sufficiently expressive of my surprise at his unpoliteness; the silent tear trembled in her eye, and, with a sigh which seemed to say, it was such behaviour as she was used to, she walked to the window. I had then an opportunity of observing Sir Henry. He was rather small in his person, his eyes black and penetrating, and his face expressive of care and discontent.

"He continued playing with the child some time; then, starting up—'Has your ladyship any commands to the St. Ledger family?' 'None, sir,' answered Lady Corbet, attempting to speak with unconcern. 'If you have, you must write to-night; as I depart for London early to-morrow morning;' then taking the child by the hand, without even bowing to me, left the room.

"The emotions Lady Corbet had endeavoured to repress, then gained the ascendancy, and she burst into tears. The subject was delicate; I, however, ventured to speak, though I could offer little consolation. It was then she acquainted me with the preceding particulars, and regretted the obdurate infatuation of her father, who had sacrificed her happiness for the possession of wealth.

"Sir Henry, as I was afterwards informed, swayed by the report which was circulated of my attentions to his lady, insisted on her accompanying him to London; and as I soon after left England, I neither saw nor heard any thing of her till about a year and a half since; when, being in London, I one morning went to breakfast with Sir John Dursley, and was there surprised by the appearance of Lady Corbet. Her dress instantly informed me she was a widow; yet, as knowing her abhorrence of Sir Henry, I was perplexed to account for the sorrow depicted in her countenance.

"The mystery was soon explained. For some time after my departure, Sir Henry's conduct and behaviour continued invariably the same, when her happiness received an additional shock, by the total alienation of his affections from his son, who, as his years and sensibility increased, severely felt the estrangement, which produced an habitual melancholy. His amusements were disregarded; company became disagreeable; and the only pleasure or recreation he seemed to experience, or would take, was in wandering through the grounds and plantations; where, when the servants his anxious mother sent in search of him, could not trace his haunts, he used even to pass the night.

"At last Sir Henry fell a victim to a decline: he still retained his dislike to his son; but, to make his lady amends, as he termed it, for the unhappiness he had occasioned her, he left her every part of his fortune, without restriction, exclusive of the family estate (about eight thousand a year) which the present Sir Henry comes to the possession of, on attaining his one-and-twentieth year.

"The attention of Sir Henry to Lady Corbet, on the death of his father, was the richest balm to her heart, and she looked forward to that happiness of which she had so many years regretted the deprivation: but the flattering illusion soon fled! Her son, on a sudden, became thoughtful, reserved, and mysterious: his answers, when addressed, were incoherent, his dress disordered, and his whole appearance indicative of internal wretchedness. He avoided his mother and passed the greatest part of his time in the apartment where his father died, and where, at last, he totally secluded himself. Lady Corbet was grieved and alarmed at this change, which the domestics openly imputed to a mental derangement; and some papers they found, nearly induced Lady Corbet to concur in their opinion. They contained unconnected sentences, which showed a mind ill at ease, if not bereft of reason.

"The mild persuasions and entreaties of his mother, were ineffectual to draw from him the cause of his dejection, which still increased; and one night, about six months after the death of his father, he privately left the hall! This circumstance was soon discovered, and the domestics dispatched in pursuit of him; but the only intelligence they could gain of him was from a peasant, who affirmed, that passing by the church early in the morning, he had seen Sir Henry ascend from the vault where the remains of the Corbet family were interred: that he was without his hat, held his handkerchief to his face, and, on leaving the church, ran with wildness across the fields toward the village. This account was farther corroborated by the sexton, who attested that Sir Henry had called him up after midnight, and demanded the keys of the church, which he did not think himself authorised to refuse.

"This information but served to perplex and raise painful conjectures in the breast of Lady Corbet: Sir Henry was not to be traced, and it was not till some time after, she received a letter from Lady Dursley, informing her of his having been seen in London. To London she immediately came, where she had been nearly three weeks, when I met her at Sir John's.

"Lady Corbet recounted these events during breakfast; and we were endeavouring to give her consolation, in a case I believe we all thought equally hopeless as mysterious, when the clerk (for my friend is in the commission for the peace) entered the room, and informed Sir John, a party of dissolute young men, who, the night before, had committed several depredations, had been conveyed to the round-house, and were then waiting at the office. Two of them, he said, who were accused as the principal offenders, entreated to speak with Sir John previously to their examination. This, Sir John peremptorily refused; and asking me if I would accompany him, we proceeded to the office.

"When I beheld the extreme youth of the offenders, (for one was not more than sixteen, the others somewhat older), I knew not whether to pity or feel indignant at their depravity. I was, however, recalled from my reflections by Sir John, earnestly inquiring the names of those who were reported as the ringleaders? The youth who had principally engaged my attention, unwillingly pronounced—'Henry Corbet.'

"'Yes,' said Sir John with severity; 'if I mistake not, it is Sir Henry Corbet!—For the respect I bear your family, young gentleman, I am sorry to see you here!'

"Sir Henry, for him it really was, shrunk abashed from the penetrating eyes of Sir John, who now proceeded to inquire into the nature of the offence.

"The constables reported, that they had the preceding night been alarmed by the cry of murder, accompanied by their nightly signal for assistance; that on hastening to the spot whence the alarm had been given, they had discovered one of their fraternity on the ground; Sir Henry had then hold of his throat—another who had a bludgeon in his hand, with which it appeared the watchman had been assaulted, had likewise hold of one arm. Several others, on the approach of the watch, fled; and those who remained, after an obstinate resistance, had been secured.

"Sir Henry denied the charge. He declared that, so far from assaulting, he and his companions had, on the cry of murder, gone to the rescue of the watchman; that his friend, St. Ledger, had wrested the bludgeon from one of the assailants, and at the moment the other watch came up, was assisting him to raise the man from the ground, for which purpose he, Sir Henry, had passed his hand behind his neck; that, without making the least inquiry, they had attacked his companions, who acted only on the defensive.

"With these particulars, he said, he wished to have privately acquainted Sir John, without exposing himself or friends to the ignorant and undeserved accusation of the watchmen.

"Sir John checked the vivacity of the youthful pleader; but as the man who had been assaulted did not appear, and the constables could not prove the defence to be false, he, after reprimanding them for exposing themselves to such night adventures, set them all at liberty, except Sir Henry, whom he desired to attend him into another room.

"Sir Henry readily obeyed, and there, with greater humility than I had expected from his late spirited behaviour, apologized for the manner in which he had been brought before him.

"Sir John admitted his excuse, and asked the occasion of his being in London? Sir Henry's face became suffused with a blush of the deepest dye, as he replied, he was on a visit at an old friend's of his father.

"'Your father,' said Sir John, 'I had not the pleasure of knowing. Your mother I sincerely respect, and as I honour myself with the title of her friend, I must insist on your passing the remainder of the day with me.'

"Sir Henry instantly assented, and continued with me, till Sir John had finished the business of the morning.

"Pleased with the opportunity, I engaged my young companion on a variety of subjects, and, though prepossessed against him by the account of his behaviour to his mother, I must, in justice, acknowledge I never met with his superior. His delivery was elegant, his judgment appeared solid, and his understanding highly cultivated: as I traced in him the resemblance of his father, I could, however, easily reconcile myself to the idea, that his mother's character of him was just.

"Sir John being by this time at leisure, we returned to Soho-square. He had not mentioned the name of Lady Corbet; and now, without any previous intimation respecting her, conducted him into the room where she was.

"I never beheld surprise more strongly expressed in the countenance of any one, than in Sir Henry's, on perceiving his mother; it approached indeed nearly to horror. As for Lady Corbet—a scream of mingled surprise and delight escaped her lips, as she hastened to clasp him in her arms; but springing on one side, he eluded her embrace, and murmuring some inarticulate sounds, attempted to rush out of the room. In this he was prevented by Sir John, who, catching him by the arm, said—'Not so fast, young gentleman. Your mother has suffered too much unhappiness by your first elopement: I shall not so easily permit you to quit her a second time. Justice has delivered you into my hands, and I resign you to her. Recollect, as your mother and sole guardian, she has an unlimited authority to control your actions?'

"Sir Henry answered, but with a groan, and clasping his hands on his forehead, seemed for some moments to struggle with contending passions; then hastily asked what was required of him?

"'Not wilfully to destroy the peace of your mother!' replied Sir John, pointing to Lady Corbet, who had sunk nearly lifeless on a sofa.

"The sight appeared to rouse Sir Henry. He flew to her, and, by the tenderest appellations, endeavoured to recall her senses. Recollection soon returned, when, clasping his hand—

"'Oh, Harry!' she cried, 'I needed not this last instance of your indifference to show how little claim I had to your regard. The ties to a mother with you are now forgotten; it once was otherwise: but Corbet will follow the steps of his father!'

"Sir Henry regarded her wildly—'My father, Lady Corbet!——' he stopped, his lip trembled, and quitting her, he paced the room with agitated steps. Lady Corbet burst into tears—.

"'Harry, do not, I entreat you, torture me with this behaviour, I have not merited it. To you I have looked for that consolation and support which, as a widow and a mother, I had a right to expect. How it has been rendered, I need not say. Silence and mystery have been the return to my solicitude—your desertion in the hour of sorrow, the reward of my tenderness!'

"Sobs impeded her utterance—she could not proceed; but Sir John, with great strength of reasoning, endeavoured to convince Sir Henry, how wrong his conduct had been, and to persuade him to act consistently with the duty he owed his mother, and to his own character, in the eyes of the world. The young gentleman listened to him some time in silence; a sigh only now and then swelled his bosom. At last, on Sir John urging him to return to Wales, with his mother, he looked earnestly in his face, and with a tone of voice highly impressive, pronounced the simple denial—'I cannot, Sir John, return to the seat of my forefathers!'

"'No!' said Sir John. 'Whither then would you go?'

"Sir Henry waved his hand—. 'The world is before me!'

"I had been, during this time, endeavouring to soothe Lady Corbet; but on hearing the replies of her son, she again hastened to him, threw her arm round his neck, and, leaning her head on his shoulder, wept in silence. Sir Henry gently disengaged himself, and reconducting her to the sofa, seated himself by her.

"'Why, my mother,' he said, 'do you wish my return to Corbet Hall? Do not, I conjure you, thus wantonly seek to plunge me into greater unhappiness. Of my wretchedness you have been a witness: of what I have suffered in my mind, you can form no idea! To me, the spot where my father expired is a place of horror—of distraction! to which, if confined, neither my head nor my heart can long sustain me in existence!'

"Sir John listened to this address with some surprise; then, shaking his head at me, pointed his finger to his forehead, as implying he thought the young wanderer impaired in his intellects.

"Lady Corbet, whose emotions had at first hurried her into the little indignant reproof I have related, with tenderness replied—she had indeed, with concern, beheld his dejection before he quitted the hall; but if any thing there had disgusted, or been the means of rendering him unhappy, she would readily consent to reside at Holly seat, or any other of her estates he chose to name, provided he would return to her protection.

"To this Sir Henry did not deign to return an answer, but, folding his arms, sat with his brow contracted, and his eyes fixed on the floor, deaf alike to the solicitations of his mother and the chidings of Sir John; nor was it till after we were joined by Lady Dursley, that he yielded an unwilling assent to our united entreaties.

"Lady Corbet's satisfaction at thus regaining her fugitive, expressed itself more in her countenance than her words: Sir Henry's was overspread with gloom; he scarcely spoke, but in the evening wrote a farewell letter to his friend St. Ledger, and early the next morning attended his mother from the metropolis.

"You will not, perhaps, Howard, wonder that the admiration I formerly evinced for Lady Corbet, should give rise to more tender sentiments, on finding her released from her vows, and at liberty to select a partner better calculated to ensure her happiness, than the one her father had chosen. I accordingly followed her to Wales, and sought the earliest opportunity to avow the state of my heart. She answered my declaration with a frankness which endeared her still more to me, though discouraging to my addresses. She never, she acknowledged, entertained but one idea of affection, and that had long since been blighted and destroyed: the happiness of her son was the only thing in which she then looked forward for her own. As a lover she could not receive me, but, as a friend, I should ever be welcomed to the hall.

"As a friend then I have visited, and am not without hopes of one day obtaining her hand. The assistance I have been able to render her in the disposal of her property, has imperceptibly worn away the reserve of our earlier acquaintance; and as I have purchased a considerable estate adjoining

Sir Henry's, I have every opportunity of increasing the esteem of this valuable woman. Sir Henry I have rarely beheld; his reserve to me has ever been in the extreme, and baffled all my endeavours to gain his friendship or confidence.

"On their return from London, Lady Corbet endeavoured to develope the cause of his conduct, but in vain. Sir Henry became again the prey of mystery and melancholy, till the arrival of some gypsies in those parts; with them he had several times been seen to converse, and, notwithstanding the vigilance of his mother, who, suspecting his intention, had appointed several of the domestics to watch him, he again, about two months since, eloped, and as it was supposed, with those itinerant outcasts!

"Lady Corbet's grief, on this second elopement of her son, was calm, but deeper than on the former occasion; all her attempts to discover him proved ineffectual, and, as a last resource, she determined on going to London to the young St. Ledger, who being the bosom friend of Sir Henry, she thought might perhaps be acquainted with his proceedings. As I was likewise going to London, I accompanied Lady Corbet, and, at her request, went with her to St. Ledger's: but that family was in equal confusion—young St. Ledger had likewise absconded!

"At that time I was obliged to leave England, therefore am ignorant how their search after the fugitives has ended. This, however, Howard, I think you must acknowledge, that Lady Corbet has far greater cause for unhappiness than yourself. You still may indulge the hope of again seeing your Ellenor—a fatal certainty assures her, she is deprived of the man she loved for ever! You never knew your son; and though you may regret the deprivation of those attentions and endearments filial affection bestows; yet you, like her, never experienced the bitter pang of having those blessings changed to unkindness and neglect!"

CHAPTER IV.

The Captain sighed—thanked Talton for his admonition—"which, if it do not carry conviction to my reason," he continued, "has at least given a clue to my ideas on another subject, and may perhaps be the means of gaining you intelligence concerning the son of Lady Corbet. Young St. Ledger, if I mistake not, is now on board, and I doubt not will give you any information in his power."

Mr. Talton expressed his surprise, and earnestly entreated to see him. St. Ledger was accordingly summoned.

On his entering the cabin, the surprise in Mr. Talton's countenance increased to the highest degree.

"Sir Henry Corbet!" he exclaimed—starting from his seat, "Good God! what is the meaning of this?"

The fictitious St. Ledger appeared equally amazed at the sight of Mr. Talton, whose name he faintly articulated, and, staggering a few paces, sunk on a chair! Mr. Talton soon recollected himself, and going to him—

"Little did I think, Sir Henry, of seeing you on board the Argo; however, as fortune has given me the opportunity, excuse me if I endeavour to convince you of the impropriety—the cruelty I must term it, of your conduct! The friendship your worthy mother honours me with, authorises me in thus speaking, independently of the duty I feel incumbent on myself, as a man whose years and experience claim the privilege of dictating to unwary youth. Beside rendering the declining days of your mother unhappy, you do not recollect the idea you are implanting in the minds of the world! In the enjoyment of every blessing affluence could obtain—every wish gratified—what could be the reason of your clandestine procedure? This is not the age of romance, Sir Henry! Your conduct, then, can claim only the excuse of lunacy!—a charge which, if authorised by a continuance of your mysterious behaviour, may, in the end, deprive you of those possessions you now appear to slight and contemn! For your own sake, I conjure you, stop ere it be too late. I shall shortly return to London; go with me, and restore the peace of your mother, whose early days, you are well convinced, were too much embittered by your father, to need an additional pang from his son!"

"He shall return," said the Captain; "at least he shall not remain with me! As St. Ledger, the victim of misfortune, I received him; as such, Sir Henry, you should ever have been welcome to my purse, my interest, and protection! As Sir Henry Corbet, the regard due to my own name obliges me to insist on your returning to your friends!"

Sir Henry's countenance underwent various changes during the speech of Mr. Talton: but the Captain's positive renunciation awakened every painful sensation. He precipitately rose, and seizing his hand—"Give not your judgment too hastily, Sir; nor deprive me of your protection before you are certain I am in reality undeserving of it!" Then turning to Mr. Talton, with a modest spirit that glowed on his cheek—

"I am well aware, Mr. Talton, of the censure to which I expose myself in the opinions of the world; but as the world cannot give me happiness, neither shall it altogether bias my conduct! You, sir, have questioned me with freedom, and now excuse me if I answer you in the same style. Your friendship for my mother, I am well assured, will induce you to acquaint her with this rencounter: I do not wish it to be concealed. Of my regard—my love, she is well convinced; and the name of mother will never let the force of those ties diminish; but tell her, till authorised by the will of my father, no power on earth shall induce me to return! Ask me not—why, Mr. Talton. There is a reason, to me a dreadful one! one—which drove me from my home, an outcast—a wretched mysterious wanderer!"

"Romance! Sir Henry," exclaimed Mr. Talton. "Your conduct has been mysterious, but you need not be a wanderer. Return to your mother—."

"Mr. Talton," interrupted Sir Henry solemnly, "urge me not! I am neither so ignorant nor weak, as to be influenced by a childish romance. I again repeat—there is a cause! If the sacrifice of my life could secure my mother's happiness, freely would I resign it: but I must not—dare not see her! My wish is to remain with Captain Howard."

"At present, Sir Henry," said the Captain, "I think it more eligible for you to be under the immediate care of the guardian appointed by your father."

"Be you my guardian," said Sir Henry, again eagerly clasping his hand. "My heart acknowledged you as such, the first moment I beheld you; when, not knowing you were the Captain Howard whom I sought, I told you my name was St. Ledger. Can you forgive the falsehood? When informed who you were, a false shame withheld me from retracting the assertion, especially as you had given that protection, as Sir Henry Corbet I should have entreated! Under that protection let me still remain! It is a child of sorrow, Captain Howard," he continued, sinking on his knee, "begs—conjures you not to desert—not to drive him again an outcast on the world!"

The Captain was affected—but an expressive look from Mr. Talton, repelled each sentiment of commiseration, and in an instant decided the cause of the supplicating Sir Henry. Addressing him with a coldness ill according with the generosity of his disposition—

"I am almost induced, Sir Henry, for your sake, to wish this discovery had not happened: as some particulars recited respecting you, by Mr. Talton, must prevent my proving the friend you wish, I certainly cannot oblige you to return to your mother—but here you cannot be till you have previously obtained her approbation."

"Recited respecting me, by Mr. Talton!" repeated Sir Henry, rising indignantly. "It is well, Captain Howard!" He was leaving the cabin, but, turning at the door, regarded the Captain with a look expressive of anguish and disappointment: the tear trembled in his eye—he faltered—"When the child of Ellenor Worton needed protection, my father did not refuse it! Edward—Ellenor!"

He laid his hand on his breast,—burst into tears—and rushed in an instant from their sight.

Surprise, approaching to agony, for a moment bereft the Captain of utterance; but, recovering, he exclaimed—

"He named my Ellenor and her child! Fly, Frederick, and bring him back. Oh God! Could he give me information of them—!"

"Be calm, Howard," said Mr. Talton. "Sir Henry, take my word, knows not of your Ellenor."

"Why then did he name her?" asked the Captain, with quickness.

"That, I cannot say:" answered Mr. Talton: "but, so well acquainted as I am with every concern of the late and present Sir Henry, the occurrence he insinuates, could not possibly have escaped my knowledge."

At that moment Frederick re-entered with a letter for his uncle, which Sir Henry had desired one of the men to deliver.

"It is from Ellenor!" said the Captain, attempting with a trembling hand, but in vain, to open it. "Take it—read it, Frederick," he continued; "I am so agitated I can scarcely support myself!"

Frederick obeyed, and read as follows:—

"After seventeen years silence, Ellenor Worton again addresses her beloved Edward—addresses him whose idea has ever lived in her heart; nor fears the world should tax her with indelicacy. It is for a child of sorrow she writes! It is Ellenor sues—nor will Edward refuse her boon!

"For reasons which I cannot explain, Sir Henry Corbet, the bearer of this letter, is necessitated to withdraw from the guardianship of his mother. His father sheltered your Ellenor and her child in the hour of keen adversity. He has equally been our preserver! To him I am indebted for the blessings I enjoy—to him, your son (Oh Edward, can you forgive my hitherto concealing him from your knowledge?) is beholden for a competency! Will my Edward repay the obligation, by affording him an asylum? From him you may learn what has hitherto befallen me; but attempt not my retreat, it must yet be sacred!

"Seek not to know more of his history than he freely communicates: and love him, my Edward, for he is worthy of your richest regard. You must hereafter clear the mysteries in which he is involved—from him it is, you must receive your son, and—Ellenor."

"But he has denied your boon, my Ellenor!" said the Captain. "Shame—shame to him for it! Yet it is not too late: seek Sir Henry immediately: my life were little in recompence for friendship shown to my Ellenor!"

Sir Henry, however, was gone!—The moment he left the letter, he sprang into a boat which was putting off for the shore; nor with the strictest search and inquiry could they trace the way he had taken. For three days the Captain experienced the torture of suspense, when he received intelligence, that the corpse of a youth, answering the description of Sir Henry, had been washed on shore about two miles from Lowestoff. Alarmed by this account, he went to the cottage where it had been conveyed, accompanied by his nephew and Mr. Talton; and where their fears were fully confirmed, by the people producing the clothes, and a watch the Captain had himself presented to the unfortunate Sir Henry: who, they informed him, had that morning been interred.

A tear fell on the cheek of the Captain as he resigned the hope so lately raised, of hearing of—and seeing his Ellenor; accompanied by one for the unhappy fate of his favourite St. Ledger: nor did the severity of Mr. Talton refuse the tribute of a sigh: the faults of Sir Henry sunk beneath the sod which encircled him, and left to his remembrance only the youth he regarded for the sake of his mother.

With his mind deeply depressed, the Captain returned on board; long had he experienced unhappiness, but the events of the last week had struck the shaft still deeper in his heart; nor could the friendship of Mr. Talton, or the affection of Frederick, preserve him from a corroding melancholy.

The death of Sir Henry, as St. Ledger, was universally regretted; even the obdurate Harland, for a moment, forgot his enmity, and expressed a sentiment of pity; whilst the generous Frederick, who had regarded him with fraternal friendship, paid that tribute to his memory his merits demanded; and whilst he dwelt with praises on the name of his friend, the faltering accent and half-suppressed sigh evinced the sincerity of his grief for his loss.

Mr. Talton finding the impracticability of his endeavours to alleviate the sorrow of the Captain, took his leave, and set out for London, to acquaint Lady Corbet with the death of her son: as, however disagreeable the task, he rather chose to inform her himself, than hazard an abrupt disclosure from an uninterested person, or even by epistolary communication.

The Captain felt relieved at his departure, as he wished to visit the grave of Sir Henry, but was unwilling to betray the weakness of his heart, even to his friend. The ensuing morning, therefore, he went on shore, and, unattended, pursued his way to the church-yard; where a simple flag of fragrant turf marked the spot where the remains of the unfortunate youth were laid.

"Humble indeed is thy bed of rest, my poor St. Ledger," he exclaimed: "by far too humble for the virtues which I am certain were the real possessors of thy breast!—In thee my Ellenor has lost the friend she too, perhaps, fondly hoped, would one day have restored her to the arms of her Edward. With thee rested the knowledge of her retreat; and with thee—it may have perished!"

The idea was too much: he sank on his knee by the grave—to Heaven his heart was open.

"Oh God!" he cried, "immutable are thy decrees, nor can the proudest knowledge of man explore the mystery of thy ways! Greatly against thee have I offended, and just is the punishment thou hast inflicted: yet still let mercy blend with thy power, nor crush the head thou hast deigned to rear from the dust! Mine was the guilt; on me let thy vengeance fall: but spare my Ellenor the anguish which swells my heart; and if thy justice prohibit more, let me at least prove (however late the date) a friend to her I deceived, a parent to the offspring of our love!"

He bowed his head on his knee, and for some minutes continued in mental supplication; till a sigh, responsive to that which burst from his own bosom, aroused him, and, on raising his head, he beheld his nephew within a few paces of the grave.

"The same reason, my dear uncle," said Frederick, advancing, "I find, has separately brought us to this spot, that of taking a last farewell of the ashes of our worthy young friend, before we bid adieu to this part of England."

"Such was my intention," answered the Captain, "though remembrance at the moment has hurried me into greater weakness."

"Regret it not," said Frederick, affectionately taking his hand. "Sir Henry was deserving of the tear you have shed!—Peace to his spirit!—Nor need we doubt it: the God to whom he is gone, will condemn or acquit us according to the rectitude of our hearts, not the frailties of our words or actions."

"That reflection may conduce more toward restoring peace to my bosom," said the Captain, "than all the sophisms of philosophy!

"But come, Frederick, you have witnessed my weakness, let me retire from this spot, or I may relapse."

He took the proffered arm of Frederick, and, giving a last look at the grave, dejectedly retraced his steps from the church-yard.

A few days after, he received his expected orders to sail for Weymouth, previously to his convoying a fleet of Indiamen to the coast of China.

A sigh swelled his bosom as he passed the cliffs of Brighthelmstone, and beheld the spot where he had once resided with his Ellenor, now lost to him, he feared, for ever. Remembrance, with keener powers, recalled her perfections; the sweetness of her manners, her chaste affection; each look, each tender endearment, dwelt on his memory, and was cherished in his heart as all that remained to him of her whom he loved. The idea of Mrs. Howard involuntarily obtruded—

"Weak man!" he softly sighed, "ever to listen to the futile reasonings of resentment! Had I not yielded to thee, Ellenor might honourably have been mine; her arms my haven, her smiles the reward of my toils and anxieties! But now—no welcome ever greets my arrival to my native shore, no offspring bless my return; Ellenor and her son are lost to me; and he who only could have restored them, has resigned his being to the God who gave it!"

Frederick, with concern, observed the increasing melancholy of his uncle, and his anxiety on that account was considerably augmented by the arrival of Mrs. Howard! That lady, whose hatred to the Captain increased with her years, no sooner gained intelligence of his being at Weymouth, than she hastened there, well knowing her presence was a far greater punishment to him than any the law could have inflicted; and as such, it proved more gratifying to her revenge than any it could afford! The Captain bore her wayward humour with apparent composure; yet it preyed on his heart, and, by forcing a comparison with the happy period he had passed with Ellenor, rendered each moment as secretly unhappy as the rancour of his wife could wish.

From this disagreeable situation he was relieved by a visit from Mr. Talton, who, on beholding Mrs. Howard, no longer wondered at the measures his friend had formerly pursued.

"Surely, Howard," he cried, "fortune has selected thee from the rest of mankind, as an object on whom to display the worst of her capricious humours. My God! what a contrast to the gentle Ellenor! I can now, Howard, more sincerely feel for your loss of her, from that I am afraid I shall soon experience myself.

"I informed you, when at Yarmouth, I had left Lady Corbet with the St. Ledger family, who were soon relieved from their apprehensions on their son's account, by his return from an hymeneal expedition with a young lady, whom they, from a family pique, had objected to his marrying; their joy, however, at his return, obliterated every unfavourable sentiment, and they received the wife of his choice with every demonstration of affection.—Of his friend, Sir Henry, he could not give the least intelligence.

"On my arrival in London, I hastened to St. Ledger's; but I cannot attempt to describe the agonies of Lady Corbet at the intelligence I brought. It appeared, indeed, nearly to shake her reason, and make her regard the relater of her son's death, as the cause of it. She instantly retired to Wales, whither I likewise followed, but could not obtain the favour of an interview. She secluded herself from company, nor admitted the presence of any one but her own servant. Thus she continued nearly a fortnight, when a report was raised, that Sir Henry had been seen in the village; and the next morning I received a message from Corbet Hall, entreating my immediate presence.

"Pale—wild and breathless—the wretched mother, on my entrance, started from her seat—'My Henry, my son!' she exclaimed, wringing her hands, 'Oh, give me back the darling of my widowed heart! It is his mother's bosom only he has wrung with anguish; he never injured thee! Why then say he is dead, why tear him from my sight? Dead!' she repeated, with a scream. 'Oh no; it was but last night he blessed my sight. Even now his accents hang on my ear, as he told me that he lived!'

"Thus she raved—and it was a considerable time before I could soothe her to any degree of composure. When I had in some measure succeeded, I dispatched an attendant to the village, to inquire into the particulars of this strange story, and, if he could possibly discover those who were said to have seen Sir Henry, to bring them to the Hall. He soon returned with an old man, who affirmed he had seen Sir Henry, or his spectre, pass down the church hill the preceding evening; that although frightened, as Sir Henry was said to be dead, he had retained resolution to follow him till he arrived at the village; but what became of him then, he could not say, as he suddenly lost sight of him.

"This account was delivered with such hesitation, I should have condemned the whole as the effect of intoxication, had not the wretched mother again declared she had seen her son! The repetition recalled her frenzy, and for some time baffled my endeavours to calm her perturbation, by assurances, if her son in reality lived, he must soon be discovered, in which case I would use every endeavour to restore him to her.

"Lady Corbet has recovered from her derangement, though I do not think she ever will from the shock occasioned by the loss of her son. She is now at Bath for the benefit of the waters: but as my presence appears to recall the fate of Sir Henry more forcibly to her mind, I have determined to absent myself till time shall have mitigated her sorrow. I cannot, however, experience ease in my present state, and must therefore seek it in a change of objects. What say you, Howard, to an excursion for a few weeks? Fortune, perhaps, may grant us intelligence of your Ellenor."

As his presence was not essentially necessary on board, the Captain readily acceded to the proposal, and a few days after they set out for Caermarthen, accompanied by Frederick.

Fortune, however, favoured not their hopes; and, after three weeks spent in fruitless inquiries, they once more directed their course toward Dorsetshire.

CHAPTER V.

Already had they reached a village near Llandaff, where they proposed to pass the night, when the fineness of the evening tempted them to enjoy the beauties they beheld in an extensive landscape. In passing along a bank from which the ancient walls of the church-yard rose, a groan, replete with anguish, assailed their ears. The heart of Frederick ever felt for the distresses of his fellow-creatures, and, on directing his eye to the spot whence the sound proceeded, a scene presented itself, which awakened every sentiment of pity.

A man, whose maimed condition implied the service he had rendered his country, was bending over a grave recently made; his hat was off, and the sun shed his last beams on a face that showed the wreck of every manly beauty, whilst his hair, gently waving in the evening breeze, shaded, and added a softness to the settled grief impressed on his countenance. A lovely girl lay at his feet, embracing the senseless turf, then raising herself, wrung her hands, and, clasping that of her companion sank on the sod in a state of insensibility!

"Ellen, Ellen, my child!" exclaimed the mourner. Frederick could refrain no longer, but, rushing through the gateway, raised the senseless Ellen in his arms. Life soon returned, when the Captain (who, with Mr. Talton, had followed Frederick) took the hand of the unhappy man; the softened accent of commiseration hung on his lips, but, the mourner murmuring an entreaty to be spared, withdrew his hand from the friendly grasp, and, taking the weeping girl by the arm, slowly directed his steps from the compassionate intruders.

His sorrow was sacred—the Captain felt it; but Frederick, whose attention was fixed on Ellen, perceiving her scarcely able to support herself, again hastened to her assistance, and the Captain waving his hand for his servant to attend him, returned with Mr. Talton to the inn.

The scene they had witnessed was too impressive to be erased from their minds; they communicated it to their host, who said—"Ah, your Honour, it was Lieutenant Booyers. Poor gentleman—he is the pity of all who know him, though I knew him when the sun rose not on a happier man: but that time is passed."

"And pray, my worthy friend," said the Captain, "to what misfortune does he owe this unhappy change?"

"'Tis a mournful tale, your Honours," answered the compassionate Jarvis, "never, I believe, did any man experience more sorrow and misfortune than he has."

"If my curiosity be not impertinent," said the Captain, "I would thank you for a few particulars respecting him. I remember a Francis Booyers, who some years since served, at the time I did, on board the Agamemnon; and what I have beheld I acknowledge has interested me. You appear to have known him long."

"From his birth, Sir: and, I believe, there are few circumstances of his life with which I am unacquainted.

"I was, Sir, in my youth a soldier, and served under the father of the gentleman you this evening beheld: as brave a man as ever fought beneath the British standard, and as well beloved by his whole regiment. During our campaign, I had the good fortune several times to gain his notice, and in the last engagement where I fought, had the happiness to save his life! It was by that, indeed, I was disabled; for I had my knee broken, and received a musket shot in my side; but that I did not regret, for, wounded as I was, there was not a man left of the regiment but envied me an action I shall ever regard as my greatest glory: Aye, your Honours, or who would not have changed situations with me, could he have said, he had been the means of preserving the gallant Colonel Booyers! I was attended with as much tenderness as our harassed situation would admit of: the Colonel himself visited me, and when I recovered, not only procured me a pension, but took me as an attendant on his person.

"Soon after, we returned to England, where the Colonel involved himself in ruin, by marrying the daughter of a poor clergyman. For his father, Lord Booyers, was no sooner informed of what he had done, than he forbade him his sight, and passed from one act of unkindness to another, till at last he disinherited him! The Colonel, at first, sought a reconciliation by means of their common friends; but, finding it of no effect, resigned all thoughts of the fortune he had expected. His lady was too amiable to let him regret the step he had taken, and, in her affection, he found a sufficient recompense for the loss of his father's.

"In the course of five years she made him the father of three lovely children, and, during that time, their happiness never received the least interruption: but our regiment was then again ordered abroad; and leaving his family in this village, under the protection of Sir James and Lady Elvyn, the Colonel bade adieu to Wales, and beneath the walls of Carthagena found a soldier's grave!

"Ah, Sir! five-and-thirty years have not worn away the remembrance of that day. Still fresh in my memory is the moment I saw him borne in the arms of the soldiers from the field. Many times had I faced death, regardless of the carnage which surrounded me—but the sight of my noble master's corpse made me a coward! The shout of victory, which had been wont to rouse me to an enthusiastic madness of joy, ceased to vibrate on my heart; and, though a soldier, I cursed the ravages of war!

"At such a time, but little ceremony can be used:—a shell was hastily prepared, into which he was laid, and the following evening carried on the shoulders of his men to the grave they had previously prepared. I followed—a real mourner! The half-suppressed groans of my comrades were answered by my own, and each stroke on the drum sank deeper in my heart. I however marched to the grave: but when I heard the earth rattle on the coffin of him, whom the day before I had beheld in the pride of health; surrounded with honour; whose words the oldest officers listened to with respect, and whose presence could animate and lead his men to the greatest dangers, then bereft of life, and hurried to the dust—to think of his wife—his children!—My heart already swelled with anguish to the utmost, could bear no more—I threw myself in the half-filled grave—in bitter terms lamented his untimely fate, and franticly accused the hand of Providence, that had not shielded him from the stroke of death! In vain my fellow-soldiers endeavoured to recall me to reason, to arouse me to a sense of apprehended danger from the scouts of the enemy: I was insensible to all but the remembrance of my master! At last they tore me from the sacred spot, and hurried me back to the battery, where I was suffered unmolested to indulge in my grief.

"Some days after, the General sent for me; he praised my honest affection, as he termed it, for my deceased master, and would have received me into his own service; but, finding me averse to the proposal, consented to my bearing the intelligence of the Colonel's death to my Lady. The property belonging to my master was therefore entrusted to my care, and I once more returned to Wales; when I found an account of his death had reached his wife by means of the public papers. She bore her loss with that meek resignation which marked her character, and, being then destitute of other support than her pension, determined, for the sake of her children, to humble herself before their stern grand-sire, and entreat his pity and protection. But his heart was too obdurate to yield to the orphan's or widow's tears; and that forgiveness he had refused to his own child, he vowed never to extend to hers.

"She then applied to his sons, my late master's brothers, the eldest of whom had a very large fortune, which he inherited from a relation: but they, like the old gentleman, were deaf to her claim of relief or protection; their pride of blood, indeed, would not let them stoop to acknowledge the poor descendants of an obscure country clergyman.

"My Lady returned to Sir James, who, on being informed of her unsuccessful application, said—'It is not more, Mrs. Booyers, than I expected from the well-known character of his Lordship and his sons: but let not this disappointment of your wishes rather than your hopes depress you. In Lady Elvyn, you have a sincere and affectionate friend: your hearts are congenial: stay then with her, and let her attentions and commiseration soothe the sorrows of your widowhood: as for your children—I will supply the place of the father they have lost.'—And truly did Sir James keep his word. My Lady remained at the Hall till her death, which happened about two years after; when she and her little girl both died of the small-pox.

"Till then I had been retained in the family as her servant: but, a few days after the funeral, Sir James sent for me into his study—'I know your worth, Jarvis,' he said, 'and respect the fidelity and attachment you have ever evinced for my unfortunate friend and his wife; and, as I believe you wish still to be near their children, I now offer you the place of butler; in which I doubt not you will acquit yourself as much to my satisfaction, as in your preceding service you did to your late master and his widow.'

"I joyfully accepted the offer, and as butler passed the remainder of my servitude.

"As for the sons of his friend, Sir James reared and educated them at his own expense, and indeed ever loved them as though they had been his own: himself had only three daughters, the loveliest girls, I think, that ever I beheld; but, alas! beauty could not secure their happiness!

"About three years after the decease of Mrs. Booyers, Lady Elvyn died: the affection of Sir James, however, scarcely allowed them to be conscious of the loss; his wife, he would say, still existed in her offspring, and for their sake he never would wed another.

"Well, Sir; early in life, Miss Mary and Hannah, the two elder, showed an attachment to the young gentlemen, and Sir James declared their want of an adequate fortune should never be a hindrance to their union with his children. For the eldest he obtained a commission in the army; the youngest had long been at sea; and, as my master's interest was great, the fairest prospect of promotion was before them. An active war then called them abroad; and well I remember the morning they bade Sir James and the young ladies farewell. My master took a hand of each, as they were preparing to step into the carriage which was to convey them away, and, pressing them to his bosom, said—'Farewell, my dear boys; and remember, whether good or ill fortune attend your pursuits in life, here you will ever meet with friends, whose hearts, proudly conscious of your real worth, will prize you for that alone. Your country now demands your services: seek then the acquirement of honour, if not of fortune; and at your return, doubt not my ready assent to the union you so ardently wish.'

"It was two years after this, before we saw either of the young gentlemen again. At that time Mr. Francis returned from Barbadoes, and Captain Booyers arrived from Ireland, accompanied by a son of Sir Horace Corbet. My old master, who had drooped in their absence, revived at their return, and for six weeks we had nought but feasts and merriment. About that time Mr. Corbet disclosed a passion he entertained for Miss Eliza; and Sir James instantly wrote to Sir Horace, who a few days after likewise arrived. Ah! all then was truly a scene of happiness!—for Sir Horace immediately gave his consent to the match, and preparations were begun for the three marriages. But, alas! Sir, nothing in this me is certain; for, in the midst of our joy, my good old master was seized with an apoplectic fit, and a few hours after expired!

"Sir Horace undertook the care of the funeral, and to settle the affairs of Sir James; but, on searching his papers, no will could be found! The whole of my master's property, therefore, went, with the title, to a distant relation; a proud sordid man, who came the day after the funeral, and, without the least feeling or ceremony, told my young ladies to provide themselves another habitation; and Sir Horace, who had pretended the greatest friendship and affection, instantly changed, and peremptorily told his son, he must cease his addresses to Miss Eliza. This, Mr. Corbet refused, and declared his resolution to espouse her, whatever consequence might ensue: but Sir Horace hurried him away to his seat in Caermarthen; nor was this all, for about a week after, Miss Eliza received a letter, as they supposed, from Mr. Corbet, entreating her to meet him at a place appointed; and my young lady, wholly unsuspicious of treachery, went without attendants (for indeed all the servants but one female had been dismissed)—and from that time, Sir, has never been heard of!"

"Not heard off!" repeated the Captain and Mr. Talton, as with one voice.

"No, your Honours," reiterated the landlord, with a deep sigh—"has never been heard of! My young master and his brother used every means to discover what was become of her; but, though they entertained not the least doubt it was Sir Horace who had trepanned her, yet, as they could not bring any proof, no redress could be obtained.

"My young ladies, being now deprived of fortune, insisted that all thoughts of marriage should be relinquished till the Captain and his brother could acquire a competence more adequate to the expenses of a family; and, finding all endeavours to alter their resolution ineffectual, my young masters at last yielded an unwilling assent; the Captain returned to his regiment in Ireland, and Mr. Francis set sail for somewhere quite the other side of the globe.

"About a year and a half after his departure, Captain Booyers was promoted to the rank of Major; when Miss Mary yielded to his solicitations, and they were married. But her happiness was of short duration: she died in less than a twelvemonth, in giving birth to a daughter!

"From that time the Major dragged on a wretched existence, till his regiment was ordered abroad, where, like his father, he lost his life in the field; leaving the little orphan Ellen to the protection of his brother and Miss Hannah.

"The Lieutenant went again to sea, in hopes of attaining a higher rank, or amassing a little fortune; without which, reason forbade his marrying to involve the woman he loved in greater difficulties: and the marriage was still and still deferred, in hopes fortune would prove more favourable; till the ship he served in was put out of commission; and, after having been many times wounded, and lost an arm, he is now returned, with no other support or reward than half-pay! Poor Miss Hannah had been in a decline for a long time; her heart, I know, Sir, was broken: she lived just to see him, and take a last farewell—and that was all!"

CHAPTER VI.

The honest innkeeper wiped a tear from his cheek as he concluded, and a pause of some moments ensued, when the Captain, addressing Mr. Talton, said—"What a character, Talton, is that of Sir Horace! My own misfortunes sink in the comparison with these unhappy people's: and I think you will allow, even Sir Henry is entitled to a portion of your pity."

"He deserves it, indeed, Sir," said Jarvis. "Soon after I settled in this inn, he stopped here on his way to my ladies; and I declare I scarcely knew him, he looked so pale and unhappy. When I told him Miss Mary was married, he started from his seat in an agony, and, wringing my hand, said, 'Yes, Jarvis, and I am married! I am married,' he repeated, 'and to one—.' He struck his forehead—walked about in great agitation, and at last, throwing himself into a chair, covered his face, and sighed to that degree, my heart ached to hear him. Poor gentleman! I never saw him after that day. Had his father possessed a heart like my old master's, they might all have been happy: but many a dark deed has Sir Horace to answer for, beside those I have related: there were his wife and daughter disappeared in a very strange manner."

At this moment Frederick entered. Jarvis, being summoned to another part of the house, made his humble bow, and left the room; and the Captain, addressing his nephew, asked if he had accompanied the Lieutenant and Miss Booyers to their habitation?

"I did, my dear Sir," answered Frederick; "and have beheld a scene equally distressing, I think, as the one you witnessed in the church-yard. I supported the lovely Ellen to her residence, and would then have taken my leave, but the Lieutenant, who I afterwards found was her uncle, entreated me to walk into the house. 'It is the abode of sorrow,' he added, 'but not of ingratitude; and never will Lieutenant Booyers turn the compassionate stranger from his gate.'

"I was easily prevailed on to enter, when the Lieutenant, opening the door of an inner room, presented to my view a lady and a youth in deep mourning. They did not perceive our entrance. The silent tear was trickling down the face of the youth; but his mother, for such she proved, wrung her hands, and, in a voice broken by sobs, exclaimed—'Oh, my Henry, to what distress has thy death reduced us!' She fell on the neck of her son, when the lovely Ellen hastening to her, with accents of the mildest pity, entreated she would be composed.

"'I could, Ellen,' answered the Lady, 'were I the only sufferer; but, alas! a prison awaits us; and my child—my Edward, what must then become of you?'

"'Fear not for me, my dear mother,' answered her son, with rising spirit. 'I will follow the steps of my brave father, and if I fall, I cannot die more nobly than in the cause of my country!' His voice, his manners, were all St. Ledger's.—By Heavens, I could have loved him as a brother!

"His mother pressed him to her bosom, but tears choked her utterance. The Lieutenant regarded her with a look of commiseration, which seemed, for the moment, to banish all thoughts of his own affliction. 'Yield not thus to despondency,' he cried, 'my worthy friend; the God whose power can calm the turbulence of the storm, and raise the sinking mariner, will never desert thee or thy offspring.'

"She answered but with her tears, when a beautiful girl, whose countenance, like the rest, bore marks of the deepest grief, entered, and in a voice, I thought, of alarm, entreated her assistance in an adjoining room.

"She instantly complied, and retired, followed by her son and the lovely Ellen.

"'Child of misfortune,' sighed the Lieutenant, 'may you one day experience happiness, proportionate to the sorrow you now endure.'

"Then, addressing me, he thanked me, in elegant terms, for the assistance I had afforded his niece: her name revived the anguish of his own breast, and, perceiving me interested by what I had beheld, he gave me the outlines of his life, a life marked, indeed, by misfortune! I thanked him for the confidence he had reposed in me, and, apologizing for the freedom of the offer, entreated to know if it were in my power, or that of my uncle, to render any assistance to the lady I had seen.

"The Lieutenant shook his head.—It was not, he said.—'Pecuniary distresses,' he continued, 'are but the secondary causes of her affliction. Early in life she lost a beloved husband, and for many years experienced the keenest unhappiness: at last Heaven sent a friend, who promised to redress the injuries she had suffered; but it was not to be: death has bereaved her of her protector; and for him it is she grieves, independently of the misery which awaits her.'

"Delicacy forbade my urging any farther, and, unwilling to intrude, I took a reluctant leave.—But, surely, my dear uncle, something may be done; theirs is not a common distress: they need a friend, and, had I the wealth of the universe—"

Frederick was interrupted by his uncle's servant, who rushed into the room with looks of the wildest delight, exclaiming—"She is found—she is found, your Honour! My Lady is now in the village!"

The Captain's countenance indicated displeasure. "Am I never to be free from the persecution of this woman?" he cried. "Order my horses; I will be gone immediately!"

"What, Sir!" said James, surprised and dejected: "not see my Lady, now you have found her?"

"Found her—found whom?" asked the Captain hastily.

"My honoured Lady, Sir; Madam Crawton, who lived at Brighthelmstone."

"My Ellenor here!" exclaimed the Captain, starting from his seat, every feature instantly illumined with joy.—"O God of Heaven! tell me where she is, this instant!"

"At the house, your Honour, where Mr. Frederick went with the gentleman and lady: I saw Madam Crawton as she came out of the parlour. I could not at the moment be certain it was her; but, willing to satisfy myself, I returned as soon as my young master reached the inn, and saw Mrs. Susan putting some parcels into a carriage. I remembered Mrs. Susan perfectly well; and at that moment my Lady came to the door. I was then convinced, and hastened back to acquaint your Honour."

The Captain could scarcely retain patience till James concluded; when, quick as lightning, he darted out of the room, followed by his nephew and Mr. Talton, and in a few minutes reached the residence of Lieutenant Booyers.

With a beating heart he raised the knocker; but all remained silent: no ready footstep answered to the summons. Again he knocked—when a peasant slowly advanced from the back of the garden, and, with a surly voice, demanded their business?

"Is Mrs. Crawton, or Lieutenant Booyers, at home?" asked the Captain.

"They are not," answered the man. "They have left the village."

"Left the village!" faltered the Captain.

"Yes," replied the man. "So, for once you have missed your aim."

"Missed indeed!" he cried. "But say—where are they gone?—Tell me, I conjure you."

"I will perish first," answered the man. "I know your business too well!"

"It is impossible," said the Captain, "you should know my business."

"Is not your name Talton!" interrupted the man.

"My name is," answered Mr. Talton. "But I cannot conceive what concern that has with the lady in question."

"A great deal," said the man. "So, once more I tell you, you have missed your aim. My lady will not go to prison this time!"

"God forbid she should," exclaimed the Captain. "Yet tell me, I entreat you—."

But the peasant disregarded his entreaties, and, again repeating his observation, pursued his way to his own home. The disappointment was too severe for the Captain to support with his wonted firmness: he sunk on the shoulder of his nephew, whose astonishment could only be equalled by his concern, at finding the house so suddenly deserted: he begged his uncle (who would have followed the peasant) to return to the inn, declaring he would himself go after him, and, either by money or threats, extort from him what he knew concerning Mrs. Crawton. The Captain complied, and, accompanied by Mr. Talton, retraced his steps to the inn, where he ordered the horses to be immediately saddled.

Jarvis (who had been informed by James, of what he knew concerning the Captain and the unfortunate Ellenor) observing the agitation of his guest, begged to know if any thing disagreeable had happened? Mr. Talton satisfied his curiosity, so far as saying, the Lieutenant and his friends, with whom they had particular business, had left the village, and at the same time asked if he knew any thing respecting Mrs. Crawton?

"There were a Mrs. Crawton and another lady, your Honour," answered Jarvis, "came here just before Miss Hannah died; but I cannot say I ever saw either of them. The young folks, (for one has a son, and the other a daughter) I have frequently seen. As for the Lieutenant leaving the village, the man must be mistaken, though he may be accompanying the ladies to their own habitation: however, if it be that which concerns your Honours, I will be bound to gain you intelligence to what part of the country they are gone, in the space of an hour."

The Captain thankfully accepted the offer, and impatiently waited the return of Frederick, who, with a dejected countenance, soon entered the room.

"I have not been able to succeed, my dear Sir," he cried; "the man is sworn to secrecy; and all I have been able to learn from him, is—they have fled, to avoid Mr. Talton and a jail."

"Avoid me!" exclaimed Mr. Talton, with surprise. "There is some mystery in this, which I cannot develope. From the time I first left England, till this evening, I have never heard of Mrs. Crawton; and to Lieutenant Booyers I am a perfect stranger."

"My Ellenor flying, and from fear of a prison!" cried the Captain. "To what distress may she not be reduced! Would that Jarvis was returned! the torments I endure are insupportable!"

Jarvis soon after re-entered—"I have gained but little information, your Honour," he began, "and that I believe not strictly true. The Lieutenant has certainly left the village. It was the appearance of you, Sir, (to Mr. Talton) it seems, which has driven them so abruptly from their home. They have taken the road to Chepstow; but whether they propose staying there, is not known."

"That information is sufficient," said the Captain. "I will instantly follow them. Let me but recover Ellenor and my son—it is all I ask of Heaven!"

Jarvis, who was liberally rewarded for his trouble, procured them a guide, and they immediately directed their course toward Chepstow. But the Captain was doomed to experience disappointment; no such carriage or persons as he described had been seen; and he could only suppose Jarvis had been misinformed, or that they had pursued their way farther into the country. Indulging this last idea, he determined to continue the pursuit; but every effort proved ineffectual to discover the lost Ellenor; and, to add to his distress, he received an express to return on board, the fleet being ready to sail.

Reluctantly he obeyed, and, on reaching Weymouth, was met by Mrs. Howard, who with increasing malignancy endeavoured to revenge herself for the temporary respite he had enjoyed. Mr. Talton accompanied the Captain on board, where, promising to use every endeavour during his absence from England to discover Ellenor, he bade him adieu, and, returning on shore, proceeded to Bath, to renew his addresses to Lady Corbet.

No particular occurrence marked the voyage: the name of St. Ledger was still mentioned with regret by the crew, and dwelt on with a painful delight by Frederick and his uncle; who passed his hours in painful retrospects, and conjectures for the present state of his Ellenor, enlivened only by the praises the friendly Frederick bestowed on the person and interesting manners of his son, so greatly resembling those of the deceased Sir Henry.

CHAPTER VII.

More than twelve months had elapsed since the death of Sir Henry, when the fleet returned to St. Helena. The pleasure experienced by his officers and crew, on attaining this favourite spot, extended itself to the bosom of the Captain: the mind of Harland too yielded to its influence; the stern contraction of his brow gave place to the smile of satisfaction, and, with a heart unwontedly attuned to cheerfulness, he accompanied the Captain and Frederick to the Governor's, where a large party were assembled, not only of the principal inhabitants, but several officers and passengers belonging to some French vessels bound for Pondicherry, and which had arrived there the preceding day.

Amongst the passengers, the Marchioness de Valois, her daughters, and a Mademoiselle de St. Ursule, claimed pre-eminence; the beauty of the latter, indeed, gained universal admiration, nor could the bosom of Harland long resist the influence of a softer passion. The Governor's nephew likewise yielded an unresisting captive to charms unequalled in the Eastern clime; and, uncontrolled by any authority but that of an uncle, whose partiality ever extenuated his faults, and exaggerated the few amiable qualities he possessed to the height of human perfection, he looked on success as certain wherever he chose to prefer his suit.

Harland observed the freedom of his addresses with an eye of jealousy, heightened by the diffidence he for the first time experienced of himself. Humbled, yet indignant, he returned on board, and hastened to his cabin; whence, in the morning, he was roused by the information, that they were to pass the day with the Marchioness, with whom the Captain had been acquainted in England.

Impetuous in every pursuit, this intelligence in an instant dissipated every mortifying reflection, and he impatiently waited for the hour which would again present the lovely Louise to his sight.

The sentiments with which she had inspired him, he attempted not to conceal; his conduct through the day sufficiently evinced them; whilst the blushing sweetness with which she permitted his assiduities, and the mildness of her manners, so different from the generality of the French, but increased the passion he had imbibed.

Though convinced she regarded the Governor's nephew with indifference, he became still more dissatisfied with that gentleman's behaviour toward her, which he found would oblige him to a declaration to the Marchioness sooner than he intended; as he wished to have been previously certified of Louise's sentiments respecting himself, and to learn from her an account of her family and connexions, with which he was as yet unacquainted. He could not, however, in idea yield to the pretensions of another, and accordingly, a few days after, took the opportunity of accompanying the Captain to the Marchioness, and, with all the energy of an unfeigned passion, declared his admiration of Louise, and entreated her permission to his addresses.

The Marchioness, imagining the declaration to proceed from a prepossession as easily eradicated as raised, answered—"That Louise is deserving of your highest admiration, I acknowledge; but her station in life is beneath what you may with justice aspire to. She is an orphan—without a name; brought up by charity, and received into my family, at the request of my daughters, as a companion: and I think, young gentleman, you must acknowledge I should ill deserve the name of patroness, if I permitted an acquaintance a few weeks must unavoidably dissolve.—As a friend of Captain Howard, and a gentleman, I shall ever be happy to see you in the circle of my acquaintance, but never as the lover of Louise.

"It is now nineteen years, Captain," continued the Marchioness, "since Louise was found at the gate of the Convent of St. Ursule: the picture, as we suppose, of her mother, was tied round her neck with a paper, on which was written the word—"Louisa!" The Abbess caused a search to be made after the parents; but, not being able to discover them, received and reared the infant. My daughters were educated at St. Ursule's, and attached to Louise from her childhood; at their request, when she was about sixteen, the Abbess resigned her to my protection."

Ill could the haughty soul of Harland brook this refusal of the Marchioness, which was beginning to raise a sentiment of indignation in his breast against that lady, when the entrance of Louise obliterated every idea but of her; each moment presented new attractions to his fascinated senses; and he determined to espouse her privately, and leave the issue to Providence, rather than forego his addresses; as love and pride whispered—her birth must be reputable, if not noble!

The day succeeding this, he accompanied the Captain and Frederick to a *fête* at the Governor's, where the Marchioness and her family were likewise present: but the pleasure Louise's presence would have created, was destroyed by the marked attentions of young Ferrand, the Governor's nephew; and, unable to endure the seeming satisfaction, or even the presence of his rival, which prevented his conversing freely with Louise, he entreated to speak with her in private, and, without waiting for an answer, conducted her into an adjoining room. He there acquainted her with his application to the Marchioness; her rejection of his suit; and vehemently urged her to a private marriage.

Louise was concerned at the Marchioness's refusal, but declared she never would consent to any engagement without her approbation; and gently chid Harland for the rudeness of his behaviour to Ferrand. Harland could not conceal his chagrin at this second rejection, and accused Louise of an unjust preference to his rival; against whom he vowed the severest vengeance.

The East-Indian, who had equally observed the assiduities of Harland, and equally felt the influence of jealousy, had followed them unperceived, and heard the whole of their conversation. He now sprung from his concealment, and would have commenced hostilities on the spot, had not the terrified Louise entreated Harland to reconduct her to the company. Though hurried nearly to madness by the violence of passion, the voice of Louise recalled him to reason; or rather her request, trivial as it was, implied, he thought, a preference to him over his rival, which, by gratifying his wishes, conduced to calm the tumult raised in his bosom.

Louise, though she had given a denial to his suit, could not behave to him with indifference: on the contrary, she endeavoured, by many little attentions, to soften her rejection, and which Harland was too happy at the moment in receiving, to bestow a thought on the motive whence they arose.

Amidst the festivity which reigned, young Ferrand was the only one really unconscious of pleasure. Ungovernable in his passions, he could as little brook an appearance of slight, as Harland could refusal. A sentiment of respect and awe he entertained for his uncle, withheld him from disturbing the mirth of the evening by an open quarrel with the Lieutenant; he therefore determined on a surer revenge than he was certain of being able to inflict with his own hand.

It was late when the company separated, and Harland, with the Captain and Frederick, were returning to the Bay, when they were attacked by four men, who in a moment struck the Captain to the ground. Harland, whose courage equalled his passions, immediately drew, as did Frederick, and endeavoured to guard the Captain, against whose life the ruffians seemed principally to direct their attention. A sharp conflict ensued, in which their assailants had evidently the superiority, and they were nearly overpowered, when a man, wrapped in a large roquelaure, hastily approached. Frederick apprehended an associate of the ruffians, but was agreeably undeceived by one of them being instantly levelled with the dust by the contents of a pistol! The stranger then flew to his side, and, seizing the Captain's sword, obliged the assassins in their turn to act on the defensive.

Alarmed by the report of the pistol, the boat's crew, who were waiting for the Captain, followed the direction of the sound, and arrived at the moment the ruffians, unable to perpetrate their design, fled; leaving their companion behind them, severely wounded.

Frederick instantly assisted to raise his uncle; and the sailors, mistaking the stranger for one of the assassins, as instantly secured him, and, finding the fort alarmed, took the Captain in their arms and returned to the boat.

When they arrived on board, proper applications were used to restore the Captain, who had been rendered senseless by the blow; and who, after assuring his nephew he was not materially hurt, inquired after the men who had assaulted them.

Frederick, whose anxiety for his uncle had till that moment precluded every other idea, immediately recalled to mind the generous stranger; and, with the warmest praises on his bravery, related the service he had rendered them. The glow of impatient gratitude for a moment warmed the cheek of the Captain, as he looked round for this unknown friend: but not discovering him, he eagerly asked where he was?—and, to his great surprise, was informed the men had confined him till his pleasure respecting him should be known.

"Merciful Heaven!" he ejaculated. "What a return!—Frederick—"

Frederick flew out of the cabin, and in a short time re-entered, conducting the stranger, who held his cloak to his face, as wishing to be concealed.

The Captain rose, supported by Harland, and, extending his hand, said—"I know not, Sir, how to offer an apology for the injurious treatment you have received, from the honest but mistaken zeal of my men, but, misled by appearance, they could not distinguish whether you were friend or foe. To the aid you so generously afforded, I am undoubtedly indebted for the preservation of my life, for which I return my most sincere thanks. Will you now inform me to whom I am thus obliged, that I may likewise by my actions prove my gratitude."

The stranger appeared agitated, clasped his hands, then, hastily advancing to the Captain, sunk at his feet, and, throwing off the roquelaure, discovered to his astonished senses—Sir Henry Corbet!

With a countenance pale as though oppressed by death, the Captain regarded him, whilst Sir Henry, seizing his hand, pressed it to his breast, and exclaimed—"Repay the obligation, then, by restoring me to that place in your friendship I once possessed, and granting that protection I still must entreat!"

The Captain endeavoured to raise and answer him, but, unable to speak, gave a faint groan, and sunk into the arms of Frederick; who, confounded and amazed at the apparition, could scarcely credit the evidence of his senses, or believe the person of his friend to be real.

Sir Henry, equally alarmed at the state of the Captain, assisted to convey him to his cabin; and, when recovered, joined his entreaties to the surgeon's, that he would seek the repose he so much required. The Captain unwillingly yielded to their solicitations; as he wished to have had an immediate explanation respecting the re-appearance of one whom he had so long thought dead; but, Sir Henry promising to satisfy his curiosity on the morrow, retired—having been previously assured that his request for protection should not a second time be refused.

Accordingly, in the morning, he attended with Frederick; and the Captain, as soon as he beheld him, gave him his hand, saying with a smile—"I find, Sir Henry, I must be doubly your debtor: your assistance last night preserved my life and now to you I must look for those blessings which can alone render life desirable. To you, my Ellenor, in her letter, refers me for intelligence: tell me then what fate she has hitherto experienced; for much I fear fortune may have in every respect proved unfavourable."

"Of Ellenor and your son, Captain," answered Sir Henry, "I have little to relate. At the time she left London with her infant, she sought the protection of my father, who procured her an honourable asylum in the family of the Reverend Mr. Blond; with his relict I believe she at present resides. Edward, when I first quitted England, was pursuing his studies at the University; which he left previously to the report of my death; and, with his mother and Mrs. Blond, fled—to avoid the unfeeling hand of oppression; but where to—I know not."

"I feared as much!" sighed the Captain.—"But Heaven," he continued with a more cheerful accent, "may yet befriend me. I have by a miracle, I cannot call it less, recovered you from the grave: and from your hand I still hope to receive my Ellenor. I am, I find, necessary to the elucidation of the mysteries Mr. Talton formerly mentioned: the friendship you have shown to my son, independently of the regard I entertain for yourself, demands from me the readiest assistance: tell me, then, what course I am to pursue, and doubt not my proving the friend you wish."

Sir Henry warmly thanked the Captain for the generous offer. "Personal protection," he continued, "is all I at present request...." He paused a moment, then again continued—"I last night, Captain Howard, promised to explain to you the accident by which you were led into the belief of my death, and, as far as I am at liberty, to relate the particulars of my conduct. Of the latter, I can say but little; and only entreat you will not judge or condemn me by appearances.

"Mr. Talton, I presume, has already acquainted you with the marriage of my parents; of which I am the only offspring: the offspring, indeed, of indifference! Since reason dawned, I have drunk the bitter draught of unhappiness: my childhood passed in sorrow; parental hatred still pursued me—and the events of one night, soon after the death of my father, I acknowledge, nearly bereft me of reason! To fly from scenes I had not strength of mind to support, I left my home, and sought relief in the bosom of friendship; till a mother's tears won me to return, when again I became the prey of midnight horrors!

"Long I sustained them; till nature sunk beneath their influence, and nearly resigned me to the grave! Again I resolved to fly.—'Seek my Edward,' said your Ellenor; 'his generous hand will sustain thee, and hereafter bear thy character open to the world!' She accordingly wrote, and, with the assistance of a gypsey, from whom I procured an humble disguise, I eluded the watchfulness of my mother, and again became an itinerant.

"I was nearly three weeks, in the weak state of my health, crossing the kingdom; as I had gained intelligence you were stationed at Yarmouth; where I was inquiring if any of your crew were on shore, when the appearance of Mr. Talton nearly annihilated me! Imagining he was in quest of me, I heeded not the answer to my question; but fled—and Providence conducted me to your nephew. Not wishing to be known to any other than the Captain Howard, whom I sought, I assumed the name of my friend, which shame afterwards withheld me from resigning, or delivering the letter I had received from Ellenor.—Refused your protection when discovered by Mr. Talton, and fearing, if persuasion failed, he would force me to return with him, I had no alternative but to leave the ship. Scarcely knowing what I did, I gave the letter to one of the men, and, hastily descending to the boat, was conveyed on shore. I pursued my way toward Lowestoff, when, recollecting Talton probably would endeavour to trace me, I changed clothes with a lad I overtook, and, giving him my watch, he promised secrecy, should any inquiries respecting me be made. My intention then was to have proceeded to Harwich; whence I thought it probable I might find some vessel going to the Continent: but, late in the evening, I was met by some smugglers. Without ceremony, they demanded who I was, and where I was going? I answered these questions to their satisfaction; when, judging by my garb I should suit their service, they, without farther interrogation, informed me I must go with them. As my life was fully in their power, I thought it most prudent to assent with an appearance of good-will, and therefore readily accompanied them on board a cutter they had lying a little distance from the shore. Our sails were immediately set, and we passed before the wind with such rapidity as soon freed me from my fears of Talton. We proceeded to the coast of Holland, where with some difficulty I escaped from my companions, and got on board a trading vessel belonging to Cardigan; and, wishing to see your Ellenor and Mrs. Blond, immediately on my arrival there set out for Caermarthen, which I reached in the evening.

"Fearful of passing near the hall, lest any of the servants should discover me, I went by the village; but, my precaution was useless: an old man, who had formerly been in the service of my grandfather, accidentally followed, and knew me notwithstanding my disguise; and, misled by the report of my death, declared to some of his neighbours he had seen my spectre! As I was hastening to the humble dwelling of Mrs. Blond, I was stopped by the appearance of Mallet, my mother's steward; and, knowing the consequence which must ensue if I were seen by him, I fled to the cottage of old Owen for shelter. Owen had that instant entered, and was relating his tale to his wife, when my re-appearance and voice convinced him of his mistake. He acquainted me with the tale which was circulated of my death, and regretted the freedom with which he had mentioned seeing me that evening: for Owen well knew the circumstances which had driven me from my home; and, as Mr. Talton was returned, advised me instantly to fly Caermarthen; promising, if any notice should be taken of what he had uttered, to conduct himself in such a manner as should effectually screen me from danger. I thanked him, and, finding Mallet was gone, hastened to the residence of your Ellenor. But, alas! Captain, it was deserted; she had left her ancient asylum, with Mrs. Blond, but a few days before! This intelligence I learned from a servant who was left in the house, and who likewise told me some particulars, that"—

Sir Henry paused—hesitated!

"I was obliged to enter the walls of Corbet Hall—what passed, I may hereafter relate; though, would to Heaven it could be for ever blotted from my remembrance!

"Spiritless and truly forlorn, every hope destroyed, I retraced my steps to Cardigan; and engaged as a common sailor, in a merchantman trading to Havre-de-Grace; but not liking the Captain, I left him on our arrival there, and led a wandering life: till I entered on board a vessel at L'Orient bound for Pondicherry; which arrived at this island with others a few days since.

"The restraint imposed on me by the presence of my messmates, was too severe to support continually: beside the anguish which preyed on my mind, my heart was with you; I wished to eradicate those sentiments you entertained from the misrepresentations of Talton, and regain that place in your friendship I once enjoyed.

"To indulge these wishes, and enjoy the freedom of reflection, I last night sought for solitude; when the clashing of swords drew me to your assistance. I first distinguished the voice of Frederick, which brought with it the idea that Mr. Talton (as he once mentioned an intention of visiting the Indies) might be with you: as the most probable means of concealment, I therefore determined on silence; trusting that in the hurry of their attendance on you, I might unobserved satisfy my suspicions, and, if they were just, escape again to shore."

"Yet, tell me," said the Captain, "on what account you so anxiously wish to avoid Mr. Talton? or why my Ellenor so precipitately fled from Lieutenant Booyers's, on hearing of his arrival in the village? He hinted that she was involved in pecuniary difficulties; to which Talton's name was annexed. Is she answerable to him for any money?"

Sir Henry answered in the negative, and begged to know what he particularly alluded to, as he had not mentioned the immediate cause of her flight. The Captain related what had passed at Lieutenant Booyers', and the idea he entertained, that Mr. Talton, notwithstanding his assertion to the contrary, had proved an enemy to his Ellenor.

Sir Henry gave a sigh to the sorrows of poor Booyers; who, he said, would prove a real protector to Ellenor till it pleased Heaven to conduct them to her. "But, alas!" he continued, "the cloud which envelopes me, likewise extends its pernicious influence to her."

CHAPTER VIII.

Frederick now turned the discourse to the occurrence of the preceding night; and proposed going on shore, to learn, if possible, who were the assailants, as he could not from their conduct think them robbers. The Captain consented; when Harland, who burned with impatience to revenge his quarrel with young Ferrand, asked permission to accompany him; which having obtained, he hastily took his pistols, and, with Frederick, was conveyed to shore.

The soldiers who the night before, on the report of the pistol, hastened to the spot where the Captain had been assaulted, found the wounded man, and conveyed him to the fort; he was there discovered to be one of the Governor's attendants: and, on being questioned, declared he had been attacked by several men, against whom he defended himself, till one of them shot him; that, as soon as he fell, the ruffians fled, imagining, he supposed, that they had effectually executed their purpose, and he was soon after found by the soldiers.

The Governor was accordingly informed of the circumstance, and ordered an immediate search to be made after the supposed assassins. At this juncture, the companions of the wounded, who were likewise in the service of the Governor, returned, and endeavoured to get unperceived to their apartment; but the blood with which one of them was plenteously bedewed, betrayed them to their fellows: they were seized, confined, and, as soon as the Governor rose in the morning, conveyed into his presence. At first they refused to answer to the charge against them; till the Governor threatened to have them instantly punished for their cruelty; when they vehemently protested their innocence; but, on being further urged, confessed they had been instigated by a considerable gratuity from young Ferrand, to undertake the assassination of Lieutenant Harland; in the attempt of which their companion had been wounded.

This, the wounded man was at last likewise induced to acknowledge; and, with great apparent contrition, implored the clemency of the Governor. That gentleman, justly incensed at this proceeding of his nephew, ordered him to be immediately called; and committed the men to strict confinement, till he should learn whether or not they had perpetrated their design.

At this instant Frederick and Harland arrived; on beholding the latter, young Ferrand turned pale; and the Governor, with some surprise, demanded an explanation of Frederick, of what he knew concerning the affair. Frederick gave an account of the assault, and concluded with the assurance, that his uncle, whom the men had mistaken for Harland, was not in the least danger. The Governor expressed his satisfaction at the latter intelligence, so much more favourable than he had expected: but, as he could not readily pardon the violent measures his nephew had pursued, he commanded him immediately to retire to his country seat: and, to prevent his having an opportunity of meeting Harland, ordered the Lieutenant instantly to return and remain on board.

Inconceivable was the rage of Harland and Ferrand at this restriction: but they were obliged to obey; each secretly tormented with the idea, that his rival would find opportunities of seeing Louise, and gaining her affections. The keen eye of jealousy had soon told Ferrand Louise preferred Harland to himself; wounded pride and indignation now led to the desire of revenge; and before he reached the abode, appointed by his uncle, he resolved to carry her off; by which means he should effectually punish her disregard for himself, and triumph over his rival. He had trusty slaves, and a retreat well calculated to secrete his prize from the knowledge of her friends and his uncle, who might otherwise severely resent his committing this second outrage.

Whilst Ferrand was settling his plan of procedure, Harland returned on board; one moment glowing with rage to chastise the East-Indian; the next, nearly frantic, lest his rank, and the interest of his uncle, should ultimately gain him the hand of Louise. The being debarred from seeing her, likewise added to the tumult of his mind; which the presence of Sir Henry, or the commendations bestowed on him by others, did not tend to alleviate.

Often in secret had he sighed for that cordiality and esteem Sir Henry experienced, instead of the cold respect with which himself was treated: but pride would not let him deviate from the conduct he had hitherto pursued; and, at the moment he regretted its influence, it hurried him into greater excesses.

In a few days the Captain, being perfectly recovered, sent an invitation to the Governor, and the principal part of the company he had met at that gentleman's, to pass the ensuing day on board the Argo: at the time appointed, the impatient Harland anxiously watched the approaching boats, and with joy perceived the lovely Louise seated by the Marchioness.

On beholding the fair European, the gaiety Sir Henry had assumed, suddenly deserted him; in vain he endeavoured to withdraw his eyes and attention from the fascinating maid; emotions but too perceptible agitated him, and the consciousness of betraying his feelings, increased them to the most painful degree.

Harland at last observed him, and jealousy whispered that Sir Henry loved Louise. The idea, in an instant, clouded the happiness her presence had given rise to; as Sir Henry, he well knew, must prove a far more formidable rival than Ferrand, whose chief recommendations were rank and fortune; but Sir Henry, to equal attractions, united a person, in which every manly beauty, fast springing to perfection, received additional lustre from an innate elegance of manners. Melancholy, indeed, had too apparently "marked him for her own," but that melancholy rendered him still more interesting.

Louise heeded not his agitation or attention, till an accident, trivial in itself, forced it to her observation, and confirmed the suspicion of Harland.

In extending her hand to re-place some fruit, a miniature fell from her bosom; Sir Henry took it up, but in restoring it to the fair owner, glanced his eyes on the features it represented. "Oh God, it is herself!"—he exclaimed, and grasped the hand of Louise—but checking the rising sentence, hastily gave the picture, and rushed past Frederick out of the cabin. Frederick instantly followed to ask an explanation, and found Sir Henry in the utmost agitation.

"For Heaven's sake, my friend," he exclaimed, "what is the occasion of this strange behaviour? Recollect yourself; nor force the company to surmises perhaps equally injurious to Mademoiselle St. Ursule and yourself. Yield not thus to the influence of your passions, or I shall indeed fear for your reason. Believe me, Sir Henry, I wish not impertinently to pry into those secrets honour forbids your revealing—yet to those you can confide, I must assert my right. You know my heart: it beats with the sincerest friendship toward you: trust it then, Sir Henry—and let it at least share your sorrows!"

Sir Henry wrung his hand—"Oh Frederick, that night—that fatal night!—and now Louise"—

"Is, I am afraid, attached to George," said Frederick. Sir Henry did not notice the observation, but continued—"Yet why should I shrink from an explanation? No—I will wait on the Marchioness to-morrow."—

"To that you must first have my consent!" exclaimed Harland, bursting into the cabin. "I love Louise; and, before I will resign the thoughts of her, I will resign my life! You had better, therefore, withdraw your pretensions."

"What means this interruption, Lieutenant Harland?" said Sir Henry. "My pretensions to Louise are founded on ties far above your power to controvert or forbid!"

Passion gleamed in the eyes of Harland; and Frederick, fearing a quarrel would ensue, entreated they would cease the subject, and return to the company: but Sir Henry declared he was too much indisposed to experience pleasure in society. Harland, whose jealousy had induced him to follow Sir Henry, to demand an explanation of his words, concluding the attempt would prove ineffectual, yielded to the remonstrances of Frederick, and returned to the gentle Louise; yet, the idea of Sir Henry's application to the Marchioness, and the fear that his overtures would be accepted, added poignancy to his torments. Harland determined, however, if possible, to frustrate his design; accordingly, as soon as the company returned on shore, he sought Sir Henry, and demanded a conference; this was refused; and he passed the night in reflections ill calculated to calm the passion which rage and jealousy had excited.

In the morning Sir Henry was taking advantage of the earliest boat, when Harland, who had been watching his appearance, hurried after him, and springing into it, declared he should not go unaccompanied. Sir Henry could not conceal his chagrin, but, seating himself in silence, they were conveyed on shore.

Meanwhile, Frederick, anxious to prevent the consequences he apprehended from the passionate Harland, as soon as he rose, went to his cabin, to exert his influence in conciliating the jealous difference: but, being informed he was gone on shore with Sir Henry, and missing his pistols, he hastened to his uncle, and, acquainting him with the preceding transactions, begged he would permit him to follow them, to prevent hostilities. The Captain said he was too well assured of Sir Henry's forbearance to fear a duel: he rather supposed they were gone to the Marchioness, whither ordering the barge, he immediately proceeded, accompanied by Frederick: but Sir Henry and Harland had not been there.

On being landed, Harland took Sir Henry by the arm, and, conducting him from the town, asked if he recollected the sentiments he had avowed the preceding evening: these the Lieutenant repeated, at the same time declaring he would oppose every pretension for the favour of Louise, and more especially from him, whom he hated!

"As I am certain, no part of my conduct," said Sir Henry, "has given just cause for your hatred, I can forgive that arising from jealousy. On no account, however, shall I defer my intended visit to the Marchioness, in which you have altogether mistaken my motive."

"Mistaken your motive!" repeated Harland haughtily. "Do you not love Louise—what other proof, then, is requisite?"

"That I love Louise," said Sir Henry, "I acknowledge; but, as we cannot agree upon this subject, I will wish you good morning." He coolly bowed, and was leaving him, when Harland, catching hold of his arm, presented his pistols, and desired he would take his choice.

"I shall not fight, Lieutenant," said Sir Henry: but Harland forced a pistol into his hand, and, retiring a few paces, fired; but fortunately without effect. Sir Henry discharged his pistol in the air, and, returning it, asked if he was satisfied? Passion had by this time so far overpowered the Lieutenant as to deprive him of articulation; and Sir Henry continued—"From my general conduct, Harland, you must be convinced it is not fear which deters me from fighting: but as you are mistaken in the motive which induces you to this action, I should think myself unpardonable to resent it, otherwise than by assuring you of your mistake. Conscious of the rectitude of my intentions, I do not fear any scrutiny you may make on my conduct; for which, if you hereafter demand satisfaction, you shall find me ready to render it, in any way you require."

He again bowed, and, repeating his salutation, walked on. "Stay! Sir Henry," vociferated Harland: "at least you shall not go alone to the Marchioness: and beware how you act; for, depend upon it, you shall hereafter render me account!"

They arrived at the Marchioness's, as the Captain concluded the account he had received from Frederick. She smiled when they entered; and Harland, with all the incoherence that anxiety and jealousy could excite, renewed his entreaties, that she would permit his addresses to Louise. He offered to settle the whole of the fortune he then possessed on her; and even to engage his parents to make an addition, if required. The Marchioness listened calmly to his offer, and gently chid him for his disobedience of the Governor's orders; but, on being farther importuned by the impatient Harland, repeated her former motives for refusing him: then addressing Sir Henry—"The same reasons, I presume, Sir Henry, will answer your pretensions."

"My pretensions, Madam," faltered Sir Henry, "are different from those of Lieutenant Harland. I seek a child, who nineteen years since was left at the gates of St. Ursule, in Rennes: whether Louise be that child, is easily known: tell me, Madam, if you have ever beheld a miniature similar to this?"

He drew one from his bosom, and presented it to the Marchioness.

"Similar to this!" she repeated with surprise. "Good Heavens, this is the miniature that was found with Louise! Tell me, I entreat you, Sir Henry, how it came into your possession; or if you know aught which could develope the mystery of her birth?"

At that moment Louise entered, and the Marchioness continued—"St. Ursule, my child, come hither. You are in the highest degree interested in the present subject. Sir Henry Corbet has brought this miniature, and inquires for a child who some years back was left at the gates of St. Ursule, in Rennes."

The colour fled the interesting face of Louise at this account: with a trembling hand she took the miniature, and compared it with that she constantly wore; the resemblance was exact. "Oh, Sir Henry!" she exclaimed;

"tell me, I conjure you, whence this picture? You seek a child—say, do you know my parents, or the reason of their cruel desertion of me in my infancy?"

"Cruel desertion indeed!" said Sir Henry; "arising from shame to acknowledge their offspring! But no longer shall you be a dependent! My heart claimed you the moment I beheld you; and a view of your mother's picture, last night, but confirmed my suspicion, that you were—my sister!"

He clasped her in his arms in an affectionate embrace, unresisted by Louise; who, surprised and bewildered at the unexpected claim, was for some moments incapable of speaking.

"Your sister!" exclaimed the Captain and the Marchioness. "Good God! Sir Henry, by what strange circumstances?"

"Seek not an explanation, now," said Sir Henry, "which must expose the frailties of a parent. The time is approaching, when every action must be revealed; but till then, spare me—spare Louise!"

Louise now disengaged herself from the arms of Sir Henry, and, throwing herself into those of the Marchioness, cried—"Oh, Madam, congratulate your Louise; she is no longer the child of desertion: she has found a relation—she has found a brother!"

The Marchioness embraced her affectionately; and Sir Henry then presented her to the Captain and Frederick, as his sister.

"And will not you too participate in the happiness of this moment?" said the smiling Louise, advancing to Harland; who had witnessed the discovery with sensations of horror rather than surprise. Roused from his torpor by this address, he regarded her a moment, then, wildly dashing his forehead, exclaimed—"By Heavens, my brain is on fire!" and ran precipitately out of the room. This incoherent behaviour of Harland repressed the joy arising in the bosom of Louise: she looked round as entreating an explanation.

"Do not be alarmed, my sweet girl," said the Captain: "these flights of Harland's are not unfrequent: reflection will restore him to himself."

The Marchioness would have urged the particulars of Louise's birth: but Sir Henry again entreated to be spared the relation, at the same time expressing a wish that Louise should accompany him to England. The validity of his claim, the Marchioness could not doubt: the account she had received of him from the Captain would not admit the idea; yet she declared she could not consent to part with Louise till the difficulties in which he appeared involved, were terminated; she would then with pleasure resign the office of guardian. With this determination Sir Henry was obliged to comply, and, after passing an interesting and agreeable day, returned with Frederick on board.

Here the servant of Harland, with a pallid countenance, informed them, his master had returned in the morning, in a state approaching to frenzy, which, after many inconsistent actions, had produced an attempt on his life! Alarmed at this account, they hastened to his cabin, where they found him in a raging fever.

The shock he had experienced on finding that Sir Henry, to whom he had avowed such enmity, was the brother of Louise, and who in all probability would have the guidance of her future conduct, was to be equalled only by the knowledge of her birth, which, contrary to his sanguine expectations, was ignoble: yet this consideration yielded to the idea, that Sir Henry, in revenge, would influence his sister against him, and perhaps withdraw her from his knowledge.

Hurried into an excess of desperation on this supposititious disappointment to his love, he had madly attempted self-destruction; in which he was prevented by his servant; but his mind, unable to regain its wonted powers, had resigned him a prey to a burning fever.

On beholding Sir Henry, every torturing reflection rose with additional poignancy: his friendly inquiries he deemed insulting, and desired to be left alone, or to the care of the surgeon and his servant. Sir Henry complied, fearing his refusal would recall that frenzy, which a few hours after returned from the violence of his disease.

For two days his life was despaired of: youth and medicine, however, prevailed; and the first object which presented itself to his returning senses, was Sir Henry performing the little offices of friendship. He shrunk from the view; but Sir Henry took his hand, and in the most cordial manner expressed his satisfaction at his amendment.

Pride, shame, remorse, and gratitude, contended a moment, for pre-eminence in his bosom; but his mind, softened by illness, yielded to the latter, and, pressing the hand of Sir Henry, he faintly said—"Why must I regard you as an enemy?"

Sir Henry, who beneath the haughty exterior of Harland's manners, had discovered the virtues which were in reality the possessors of his bosom, though warped by the prejudices of education, answered—"Put me to the test, and let me prove myself a friend! Not my actions, but the passions of Harland, have induced him to entertain the idea: would he yield to the philanthropy nature implanted in his heart, and regard mankind as worthy his esteem, Corbet would indeed hail him as a friend and brother!"

The word Brother occasioned a tumult in the breast of Harland, which the surgeon observing, insisted on their ceasing farther conversation; and Sir Henry soon after left him to his repose.

From this time Harland rapidly recovered, and a few days after ventured to mention Louise. Sir Henry assured him of his ready concurrence in his addresses to his sister; and, observing a latent spark of pride rekindling at the idea of her birth, said—"The circumstance of Louise's birth cannot, I admit, be justified: but reason, if not love, will acquit her of the fault and shame which must reflect on her parents. Her intrinsic virtues have gained her the admiration and friendship of her own sex; can ours then hesitate a moment in acknowledging them? And remember, if it were not originally for their virtues, we should none have cause to boast of our ancestors." Harland acknowledged the justness of his observation; and Sir Henry, at his request, undertook to plead his cause to the Marchioness and Louise.

The Marchioness no longer objected to his addresses; more especially as the anxiety Louise had experienced during his illness, convinced her he was not indifferent to her. Harland, therefore, had permission to visit as an accepted lover; the Governor, unapprehensive of any further danger respecting his nephew, readily consenting to free him from his interdiction.

With an exultation he neither strove to repress, nor wished to conceal, Harland received the intelligence of his enfranchisement, with the Marchioness's invitation; nor would the Captain, by unnecessary delays, add to his impatience to behold Louise. Sir Henry was with his sister; the Captain and Frederick therefore accompanied him to the Marchioness's.

Louise, now authorised by her patroness' as well as Sir Henry's approbation, received Harland as the lover of her choice: and his entreaty that she would unite her fate to his before they quitted St. Helena, was no longer refused. Louise was too ingenuous to conceal the sentiments of her heart; and as she presented her hand, the chastened delight which sparkled in her eyes, and the blush that suffused her cheek, told a tale to Harland, which amply compensated for all the anxiety he had suffered on her account.

At his ardent request, the Marchioness appointed an early day for their nuptials; and Harland, more enamoured than ever, in the evening bade adieu to Louise, and returned with the Captain and his youthful companions on board; his heart replete with every pleasurable sensation that love and the gayest illusions of hope could inspire. But short was his promised happiness—the succeeding morning, on going to the Marchioness's, he found that worthy lady and her daughters in tears, and the family in the wildest confusion: Louise was not to be found; nor could the least trace be discovered to direct them to the place where she had fled, or been forced!

"I have dispatched a servant for Captain Howard and Sir Henry," said the Marchioness, still weeping; "and have likewise sent for the Governor; as I strongly suspect it to be Ferrand who has torn the sweet girl from my protection."

The name of Ferrand recalled the suspended faculties of Harland: his brow contracted, fire flashed in his eyes, and in dissonant terms of the maddest passion, he vowed the destruction of his rival!

At this moment the Captain and Sir Henry arrived: the pallid countenance of the latter spoke more forcibly than language his concern at this accident, as, with trembling lips, he entreated the Marchioness to explain the particulars of the account they had received from the messenger.

Little intelligence could be given.—Louise had, the preceding night, retired to her usual apartment; but in the morning the Marchioness, surprised at her non-attendance at her toilet, (a duty Louise had never neglected) sent one of her daughters to inquire if she were indisposed, who immediately returned with the account, that she was not in her room, nor, from the appearance of the bed, had it that night been slept in; one of the windows was likewise open; and, from the disorder of the furniture, and a handkerchief Louise had worn the preceding day lying on the floor, torn, they had every reason to suppose she had been forced away.

The relation of these circumstances increased the frenzy of Harland, who would that instant have gone in pursuit of Ferrand. Sir Henry started up to accompany him.

"This madness must not be," said the Captain, detaining them. "Though suspicion points at Ferrand, you are not certain he is the aggressor; and if he be, it is to the friendship of his uncle you must look for redress: do not then, by an avowed act of violence, induce him to espouse the cause you want him to condemn. But here comes the Governor; and I beg, Harland, you will at least restrain your passion, and hear his opinion, before you determine on your procedure."

Harland's feelings were at that moment too tremblingly alive to the insults Louise might experience, to admit the reasonableness of the Captain's request. Louise was the prize on which he had fixed his happiness; nor could he, with even an appearance of indifference, see a man so nearly related to him, who had torn her from his arms. He could not, however, reply, as the Governor was that instant announced.

On being informed of their distress, that gentleman expressed such a generous concern for the occasion of it, as nearly disarmed Harland of his resentment. He assured the Marchioness, if it were his nephew who had committed the outrage, Louise should be restored; as, independently of her prior engagement to the Lieutenant, and amiable as he acknowledged her to be, he did not wish Ferrand to form an alliance with her. That no unnecessary time might be lost, he ordered two of his attendants to proceed immediately to his countryseat, with orders, if Louise had been carried there, to reconduct her to the Marchioness. The impatience of Harland could be no longer restrained; he entreated the Governor would permit him to accompany the messengers. No one, he pleaded, was so interested in the issue of the search as himself; no one, then, so proper to undertake it.

"I cannot grant your request, Lieutenant," answered the Governor, "however I may wish to oblige you; as the life of my nephew might be endangered by my compliance. I know his disposition—I have had proofs of yours: nor dare I trust you in the presence of each other. If it will be any satisfaction to you, Sir Henry may go; and if he be unsuccessful in his mission, you shall have full liberty to search any, or every part of the isle, except the spot where Ferrand is."

Harland thought the restriction unjust; but the expressive eye of Sir Henry checked the impetuous sally of his impatience.

"The anxiety I feel for the recovery of our Louise," said Sir Henry, addressing him, "can be exceeded, Harland, by none but your own: and for the permission offered me of accompanying the messengers, I accept it with thankfulness. You, Harland, will remain with the Marchioness till my return; when if I be unsuccessful, we will proceed on a further search."

The brow of Harland was still contracted: a darkened passion rolled over his soul: his eye glanced to the Governor, who was conferring with the Marchioness and the Captain. Sir Henry read the tumult of his mind, and, drawing him aside, endeavoured to reconcile him to the Governor's commands.

"And what," answered Harland vehemently, "must Louise think? To be rescued from the hand of villany—perhaps of dishonour, by the hand of a brother, or menials, whilst he who nearly claims the name of Husband stands by like a dastard, in the moment of danger! By Heavens, Sir Henry, it must not—shall not be!"

"It must, Harland," said Sir Henry. "In this respect the Governor's will is law: and Louise is too just—too generous, to impute to you as a slight, that which proceeds from necessity. Then cheer up, man; in a few hours, I trust, all will be well."

A servant now entered, to inform Sir Henry the attendants were waiting. He shook Harland by the hand, and, taking a hasty leave, set out for the Governor's seat.

END OF VOLUME I.

Milton Keynes UK
Ingram Content Group UK Ltd.
UKHW012314040624
443649UK00007B/639

9 789361 473807